LANDSCAPE FOR MURDER—

"It's Steve, Mrs. Chapman. He isn't dead! He's alive—here in the park."

She stared at me silently for a moment.

"You're perfectly mad," she said. "Steve was killed in a motor accident three years ago . . ."

This turn in the road through magnificent Yellowstone Park leads the unwary victims through a landscape of mystery and suspense. A murderer awaits them in the beautiful—but treacherous— shadows.

OLD
LOVER'S
GHOST

By LESLIE FORD

WILDSIDE PRESS

Published by Wildside Press LLC
www.wildsidepress.com

To Tom Gill who suggested a Yellowstone job

*To A. E. Demaray, Associate Director of the
National Park Service, and E. B. Rogers,
Superintendent of Yellowstone Park, whose
help and kindness made it a pleasure*

1

It was Cecily Chapman's extraordinary grandmother who insisted on that three-day pack trip from her ranch into Yellowstone Park. Perhaps the idea hadn't occurred to her, originally, that once we were there somebody was bound to push George Pelham into a boiling geyser hole. It must have more than once, before we passed the boundary Ranger Station in the wilderness they call the Thorofare. It certainly did to the rest of us—my seventeen-year-old son Bill, myself, Grace Latham, and Joe Anders the wrangler-guide, to say nothing of the camp cook and practically all the horses.

And Mrs. Chapman had sounder reasons to object to George Pelham than the rest of us. It was her granddaughter he wanted to marry. He'd been trying to, so far unsuccessfully, for some time—in fact ever since Steven Grant, the man she'd been engaged to, had died three years before. Mrs. Chapman had told me that briefly the first fifteen minutes after she'd met me at a hot dusty railroad station somewhere in the sage brush of Wyoming. "And frankly, my dear," she'd said flatly, "I wouldn't have Cecily marry that spoiled arrogant young man for all the tea in China."

I'd looked at him, large and blond and quite good-looking in Western clothes, amiably helping Bill get my luggage off the platform into the station wagon. I'd thought he was nice, if very Eastern and rather too Harvardish, in his new cowboy hat and shiny Western boots. And glancing surreptitiously at my hostess I wasn't too sure about her. She looked pretty grim to me. She was a square-figured, square-faced, white-haired old dowager, seventy at least, in an amazing

outfit of a battered ten-gallon hat and specially cut riding **skirt** of blue denim faded to the same pale blue as her frosty **old** eyes. The way she handled the station wagon on the three-hundred-mile drive to the Cinnabar Ranch, as if it was an unbroken cayuse, hadn't dispelled any of my misgivings either. Only the fact that my son Bill, who'd spent the summer at Cinnabar with her grandson, who was a classmate of his at St. Paul's, simply adored her made me hesitate about judging her from her first astonishing appearance.

And Bill didn't like George Pelham either. He hadn't said so, in so many words, in his brief curiously spelled communications home. Cecily was "tops," so was her grandmother. George he'd barely mentioned. But I could tell instantly by the stiff self-conscious way he tried to do my luggage without George Pelham's help that there was something he didn't like.

Then at the ranch I'd seen Cecily. She was slim and brown as an Indian, with curly short-cropped burnt-sugar hair and eyes the color of dark amber flecked with gold. She may have been twenty-three, but she didn't look a day over eighteen —except, oddly enough, when she looked at George Pelham. Then something seemed to happen to her face. Her eyes that lighted up like stars at everybody and almost everything, from the ranch cook to a tame ground squirrel begging for food, didn't, so instantly and impulsively, for George. It was almost as if some profoundly disturbing question about him pulled like a powerful undertow beneath the surface of her mind. It didn't seem to be something she was fighting so much as something she was trying to understand and resolve, perhaps, before she decided she'd marry him.

I was pretty sure she wouldn't, after a little, and by the time we got to the boundaries of Yellowstone I was convinced of it. I was also convinced that that was why Mrs. Chapman had insisted on the trip. There's something astonishingly revealing about people in the wilderness, and Mrs. Chapman knew it. There wasn't any other reason why she should have decided to go to Yellowstone. She'd been there a hundred times. Cecily didn't want to go, particularly, and George Pelham definitely preferred not to.

As for me, I was going because my old friend Colonel John Primrose (92nd Engineers, U. S. A., Retired) had persuaded me that since Bill was in Wyoming, and Yellowstone was definitely part of every American child's education, I ought to take him to see it before he went back to school. He didn't tell me until the day I caught the plane for Denver that the

Army had once held Yellowstone against poachers and tourists, and that that was where he and his self-styled "functotum" Sergeant Phineas T. Buck (92nd Engineers, U. S. A., Retired) had met and started their long and profitable association in war and crime.—Or that they'd already decided to make a sentimental pilgrimage back, and were in fact practically ready to start the next day.

I suspect he didn't even then tell Sergeant Buck he'd sold me the well-known line of America for Americans. If he had, their car would never have made it. It would have broken down, totally and irremediably, somewhere east of the Missouri. I can't, just off-hand, think of any holds that Sergeant Buck would bar to save his colonel from a designing widow and the fate far worse than death. I'm very sure the nearest thing to expression I ever saw on Sergeant Buck's granite-fissured visage was the afternoon we walked into the lovely sun-splashed lounge of the Lake Hotel and he realized I'd relentlessly tracked them down to the furthermost corner of the globe.

He sat rooted to the deep padded wicker chair, paralyzed with consternation. Then he heaved his six-feet-three and two hundred and twenty pounds out of it with a kind of disgusted resignation. His viscid fish-grey eyes, as warm as ice, travelled up my blue jeans and rested on my sunburned blistered nose.

"*We* thought you was somewhere in Europe, ma'am," he said sourly, out of one corner of his mouth.

"You mean you wish I were," I said, with false cheerfulness.

But that was later. Coming down the steep trail along Lynx Creek from Mariposa Lake across Two Ocean Plateau, I hadn't been thinking about either of them. Not since the day I'd told Mrs. Chapman we couldn't possibly stay another week because I'd arranged to meet friends (it seemed more proper that way, even if calling Sergeant Buck a friend was little short of slander) at Lake Yellowstone the following Monday. That was when she decided we'd all go, and we'd take a pack string because it would be fun for Bill. He hadn't been on a pack trip.

Her faded old blue eyes had brightened as she looked at George Pelham.

"In fact," she said, "I wouldn't be surprised if it wasn't fun for everybody."

I suppose it depends on what you call fun. She and Bill certainly loved it. My nose got blistered, muscles I never knew I had, from riding ordinary Eastern horses, creaked and groaned. But sleeping by a lake under the vast black gold-dusted sky, with the tinkle of the lead horse's bell coming fitfully from the meadow, was all very special, and infinitely remote from the rumors of war and the headlines of war that I'd left in Washington. So was waking up with the gorgeous smell of coffee and frying bacon, and the sun just over the rim of the dun-colored mountains, and the crisp light air fragrant with pine.

It really was fun. I didn't mind George Pelham's daily complaint that the cook purposely tipped over the can he was heating his shaving water in. Nor the fact that Bill never seemed to hear George asking him to fetch another—not until Cecily would say "Let me. I'm going to get some anyway." Then Bill would go along, and George would wait, sniffing at the bacon and coffee, warming his hands at the fire, and say "Oh, thanks very much," as if it had been their idea, not his, in the first place. Only Joe Anders, at the improvised corral fence, would glance back from feeding the horses their bucket of oats, look at him silently for a moment, and turn his sealed poker face back to his job.

It wasn't that George Pelham couldn't be a completely delightful person when he chose to be. The first two days I'd known him I'd thought he was one of the most urbane and charming people I'd met for a long time. Mrs. Chapman's pungent analysis of him I decided was not unnaturally prejudiced. I put Bill's comment, when I asked him how he liked George and got a brief "He's awright, I guess," down to the fact that Bill was seventeen and about as urbane as a cub bear, and Cecily didn't have as much time, any more, as she'd had before George came out. But about the third day I began to understand what they meant. In a hundred small ways and a few not so small, George Pelham's chief and absorbing concern was for the ease and comfort of George Pelham. Not blatantly at all, but with the quiet and single-minded conviction of an only son who thought the world was a larger circle of mothers and sisters to wait on him, and mop up after him, and put adhesive tape on his minor cuts and scratches.

It hadn't taken long to see that a state of armed neutrality existed between my son and George, except that George didn't know it. Before we started on the pack trip it had extended to Joe Anders and the cook, and after the incident of the palomino it broadened definitely into what Sergeant Buck, with his genius for language, calls "gorilla" warfare.

Mrs. Chapman had told George positively and flatly he couldn't take the palomino; she was afraid for even Cecily to ride him. George had taken him anyway. Worse than that, instead of staying decently in the pack train he'd galloped him off ahead as if he were leading a Polish cavalry charge. Later we saw, from the tell-tale evidence in a shallow creek bed, that he'd been thrown. When we finally came up with him, he was sitting under a lodgepole pine, the palomino, his cream-colored flanks dark with sweat and twitching with excitement, tethered to another. George got blandly up and said, with never a word about his accident, "Cecily, what do you say we swap horses until lunch?" For a moment Joe Anders's eyes were burning pin points, and I thought Mrs. Chapman was going to forget that three-fourths of the year she's an Eastern lady. But she didn't. She merely said, "I don't want either Cecily or the horse killed, George. We'll leave him at the Bar U D when we go past. Joe'll take care of him now—you can ride Sandy." It was perfectly urbane on the surface, but the surface was thin.

It got thinner Saturday night after we'd got into the Park, passed the padlocked and shuttered snowshoe cabin the rangers use for shelter in their winter patrols along the boundary, and camped about five o'clock at Mariposa Lake just west of Two Ocean Plateau. We planned to camp there all night, cross the Continental Divide the next day and go down into the valley of the Yellowstone to register our entrance into the Park officially with the Ranger at the Thorofare Station.

Mrs. Chapman and I were sitting on a fallen tree where we'd pitched camp. Wood for a fire was piled the ten feet from the water that our permit required. The rest of them had waded out into the lake in hip boots and were fishing for supper.

"Remember five's the limit," Mrs. Chapman called out after them. "George, of course, knows you fish with a fly, not a spinner," she added to me, sardonically.

As fishing is something I don't know anything at all about, I just nodded. I'd heard that Mariposa Lake was so full of fish they got in each other's way, what with the government stocking it every year and very few people ever reaching its wilderness calm. It must be true, because it seemed practically no time before Joe and the cook and Cecily and Bill had caught their limit, and we had all the fish we could possibly eat. George had one, and it was too small to keep, and he was taking it with ill-concealed bad grace.

Cecily's "Come on in, George, we've got loads," didn't in

the least help matters. He reeled in his line and took off the fly.

"Bring me a spinner, Bill," he shouted.

Bill, squatting on the shore with Joe and the cook, cleaning his catch, didn't even hear him. The gulls that had flocked, squalling and screaming and swooping like carrion crows, may possibly have drowned him out. Anyway it was Cecily who waded out and took him the spinner, and brought his elaborate fly book back to his kit.

Mrs. Chapman watched her with a curious little smile in her eyes.

"I wish I could figure Cecily out," she said slowly. "I can't believe she's in love with that man. Have you ever noticed the way she looks at him?"

I hesitated. It was one of the first things about her that I had noticed, but I didn't like to say so.

"Well, just watch her some time," Mrs. Chapman said. Her eyes were following her granddaughter dashing gaily back to the fish-cleaning brigade.

"Maybe it's just what they call wishful thinking on my part." She shook her head. "—I wish Steve had lived," she said, after a moment.

"They were engaged, you said, didn't you?"

She nodded.

"Who was he?" I asked. I'd never seen her in this softened mood before, and I was curious.

"It was the boy-next-door sort of thing. He and Cecily's cousins were the same age. He used to come out here in the summer with them. He was a lot like Bill—blue eyes, and hair like a straw stack, and the same kind of grin. Cecily was a ratty carrot-topped child. I'm sure the only reason all her aunts and uncles put her down in their wills was because they thought she'd never get a husband unless the pill was sugar-coated."

I looked down at the slim lovely girl in blue jeans squatting down watching them filet the sleek cutthroat trout, throwing a tail laughingly to a brown young seagull excluded by his betters. The setting sun burnished her bright hair to molten gold. Her eager sun-tanned face with its pointed upturned chin and sparkling wide-set eyes was enchantingly radiant.

"Anyway, Steve Grant fell in love with her, gangly and snub-nosed as she was. That was the summer she was sixteen. It was very silly and quite sweet, and none of us thought it would last. Then all of a sudden, just before she was eighteen, she came home from school the loveliest thing you've ever seen. That's when George Pelham met her. He was twenty-nine, and a junior in her father's office. He gave her a terrific whirl when she came out, and Steve was scared to death of her."

Mrs. Chapman laughed.

"He was twenty-four and working like a beaver. I'll never forget the weekend he came down from town to her party at my place. He just sat in a corner and let the stag line stampede her. I could have slapped him. I'm sure it was Cecily who made him remember he promised to marry her. He was in her father's office too. When they announced their engagement he acted exactly like a man who'd had a star fall in his hands and not the slightest notion what to do with it."

She smiled, shaking her head slowly. Then her face clouded.

"He got infantile paralysis, that spring in the south on some business for Cecily's father," she said softly.

"How *awful!*"

"It was awful, for everybody, except Cecily. She was superb. She never wavered an instant. We didn't know, at first, of course. Then it seemed too marvellous. After a year he came back to New York so much better than any of us had dared to hope. He was wonderful about it. And then— it was too ghastly. I went up to Cecily's room one Sunday night to see if a new maid had turned down the bed properly. I switched on the light, and there was Cecily in a heap on the floor in a storm of tears. All I could get out of her was that Steve had left. The next morning they found his car, with him in it—burned and twisted and tangled, up against a telephone pole eight miles from our entrance."

She stopped. Her eyes were fixed on a distance far beyond the narrow reaches of the lake.

"How it happened no one can ever know. After the awful struggle he'd been through it seemed so terrible, so useless; . . . oh, *so* useless."

She stopped again. When she went on her voice wasn't as steady as it had been.

"What happened between him and Cecily that sent him off that way I've never known. Cecily never said a word about it. I know that night after I'd got her to bed I went back to look at her. She was at her desk. She looked up, her face so white and stained with tears that it was heartbreaking. She said, 'I'm writing to Steve. I can't let him go, Granny—I love him too much.' —The next morning they brought us the news from the village. Cecily was bringing the letter down

11

to go off in the morning post. She didn't make a sound. She just stood there, clinging to the bannister the longest time. Then she turned around and went back up the stairs—so slowly I thought she'd never reach the top. I can still see her . . . and see her on the floor in front of the fireplace in her room, watching the letter with all her heart in it curl up and die in the flames. It seemed as if everything that made her so vivid and alive and lovely died with it.—All the quicksilver quality that made her so . . . so unpredictable on the surface, but for us who knew her never touched the stanch loyal core inside her . . ."

Mrs. Chapman shook her head, her eyes on the girl by the lake side.

"She never mentioned Steve's name again—not once in those first dreadful months when we didn't know whether it was her mind as well as her heart that had suffered.

"Then one Sunday night, almost two years ago now, George was down. He'd been extraordinary through all of it —during the year Steve was away and after the accident— but he was getting impatient, I think. He'd talked to her father about marrying her, but he'd never spoken to her. They were playing Chinese checkers in the back drawing room. All of a sudden I saw Cecily get up. She was like a flame shooting up from something no one could guess was smoldering. I heard George say, 'Well, my dear, ask your father. I'm not trying to hurt you, but I think it's time——'

"I'll never forget it. Cecily flew through the front room where I was reading without even seeing me, and into the library, George at her heels. I heard her 'Father!' and the door slammed shut. I stood it as long as I could, and I went in. Cecily was standing on the hearth rug, her face as white as snow, those eyes blazing.

" 'I'll never believe it, never—never! You're horrible, both of you!'

"Her father got up and went over to her. She turned on him—and she adores him. 'Don't you dare touch me—I hate you!' She was past me through the door like living wildfire. After a while her father looked at George. 'Perhaps it was wise to tell her,' he said. 'Perhaps the shock—. I don't know. We'll have to wait and see.' He turned to me. 'It's nothing, mother—nothing that's ever to be spoken of again. Understand that, please, George. And I think you'd better not try to see her again, for a while."

Mrs. Chapman paused again, a long time.

"It may have been the idea that it was suicide. I don't

know. I didn't try to find out. I only know that I don't believe it. Steve was impulsive and hot-headed and he'd been
through hell enough for half a dozen men. If it was—and
nothing will ever make me believe it—the provocation must
have been desperate indeed. I only know that whatever it
was, Steve couldn't do anything ungallant, or dishonorable,
or disloyal. He was the finest human being I've ever known
or hope to know. That's why I don't want Cecily to marry
George. He's spoiled and self-centered, and he'll never be
very much in love with anybody but George Pelham. Cecily
needs—and deserves—all the understanding and devotion
that only some one very deeply in love with her can give.
She's just regaining some of her old prismatic quality, the
last few months—I don't want anything ever to destroy it
again."

Just then a jubilant shout came from out in the lake.
George was pulling in a shining fighting sheath of silver.

"I've got my limit," he cried. "They're bigger than yours,
Cecily."

He came bounding in, triumphantly waving his string.

Through the pine-scented smoke of the fire where Cecily
and Bill were helping the cook I saw her look around, her
face clouded.

"That's swell," she called. "But we've got more than
enough now."

"I'll eat 'em, don't you worry," George said. He held them
out. "Here, Bill, clean 'em for me, will you." He tossed
them across the grass. "And don't get 'em mixed up with the
others. They're mine."

He turned around. "Where's my case?"

I looked at my son. His undistinguished young face was
the most extraordinary object in that line that I ever hope
to see.

"Oh, *dear!*" I thought.

Mrs. Chapman got sharply to her feet. "Who catches 'em,
cleans 'em, George," she said brusquely.

"I'll give you half a dollar, Bill," George said cheerfully.

I didn't dare look at Bill then—I really didn't. I saw Cecily
spring to her feet and pick up the string.

"I'll clean them. I love to clean fish."

Bill got up, walked over and jerked them away from her.
"You'll get your hands dirty," he said stiffly. "I'll clean 'em.
But you can keep your tainted gold, Pelham," he added, with
remarkable sang-froid.—Only it was the first time he'd ever
called an older man by his last name alone.

Cecily glanced quickly at George Pelham looking aimlessly about for his rod case. A curious shuttered look dimmed her live sensitive face. She walked over to his khaki roll, lying just as he'd left it, picked up the case and threw it to him without a word. Then she turned and ran down to the water after Bill. I couldn't hear what she said to him, but I saw him flush, look at her and grin, and hand her a fish tail to toss to the gulls who'd all come screaming back again.

It was inconceivable, just then, to think that here in the heart of this wilderness anything could happen that would make all these things trivial and unimportant and wipe them completely out of Cecily's mind. Yet within forty-eight hours something had happened—and in less than half an hour after Cecily became aware it had happened she was standing in front of Mrs. Chapman, her face pale, her head high, her voice perfectly calm. "—I'm going to marry George, grandmother, the end of the week—as soon as I can talk to Dad." But at this moment, with the setting sun streaming its flaming banners across the lake, I wouldn't have believed it possible. Even later, when I knew it might so easily happen, and held my tongue when fear almost made me speak, I still hoped—and desperately—that it wouldn't happen . . . not that way.

2

Not, of course, that George Pelham wasn't by all ordinary Eastern standards eminently marriageable. He was. It was just that the square old lady in her extraordinary Western regalia and her high-heeled boots stamping down to join the two of them cleaning George's fish had about as much use for ordinary standards, East or West, as the large antlered bull moose peacefully grazing, eye-deep in the water, at the other end of the lake. And I should have thought the same was true of her granddaughter, looking up eagerly as the old lady squatted down beside them on the shallow beach.

I'm not quite sure how the matter of George's financial prospects had come up during the first couple of days I was at Cinnabar. Money, or lack of it, is usually the chief objection that most of the people I know have, when they do object, to a man who wants to marry their daughter. And *vice versa,* except that it's not so baldly stated. Possibly Mrs. Chapman thought that was what I was thinking about her opposition to George. And possibly it was. Anyway, she'd said, quite abruptly, one evening when we were alone,

"Money has nothing to do with this, Grace. His mother left **him** everything she had, and he's done very well. Cecily's **father** thinks he's unusually able—wonders why he stays with him when he's had better chances. Doesn't see Cecily's the reason. Fathers are all as blind as bats."

She gave a kind of muted snort.

"His father made a sizeable fortune out of some corrosive people drank during Prohibition when they couldn't get liquor. Supposed to be medicine. He got out in time and put the money in respectable commodities, so the Pelhams don't have to be ashamed of it any more."

"Is his father dead?"

She nodded.

"I didn't know him, but I suspect he was a very shrewd old man. He took one look at his daughters' suitors and announced the estate was to be kept intact until the youngest grandchild was twenty-one. That thinned out the ranks enormously. As a result they both married quite well—no divorces, nice families. The two girls were a good deal older than George. May, the elder one, married Alexander Ridley, of Ridley and Hall in New York. Anna married a mining engineer and lives in Mexico. They have one son who finished Princeton two years ago. The Ridleys have two children— Philip, who's Cecily's age, and Lisa, who's nineteen.—So in a couple of years they'll all be very well off, with the additional advantage of having had to help shift for themselves. And as a family they get on remarkably well with each other."

I was thinking of that, there by the lake, just as George Pelham, having zipped up his rod case, sauntered over to where I was sitting.

"Aren't you all in?" he asked, flopping down. "I am."

He stretched out full length on the grass, crushing a small blue sea of harebells and gentians.

"It's swell out here, isn't it? This is my first trip west. I was coming out one summer with a fellow in the office. He got infantile, so it fell through. I went to Paris instead."

I just stopped myself from catching my breath sharply. It seemed so heartless and casual, some way, after all Mrs. Chapman had said with so much feeling, that I was a little shocked. George must have sensed it. "He got all right," he added. "Then he got killed in a motor accident. A lot of people thought it was suicide, and I guess it was, as a matter of fact. You never knew him, did you? Steve Grant?"

"No," I said.

"It's funny, about a guy like that."

He sat up and fished a pack of cigarettes out of his jeans.

"I've always thought maybe it affected his brain. I know it's not supposed to, but he did some of the damnedest things. We had a clerk in the office—Johnny Brice, his name was. His father was in a sanatorium for incurables. One Saturday noon he just up and quit. Nobody could figure out why. We never did, until Steve was killed."

He lighted his cigarette and tossed the match aside into the dry grass. Joe Anders, who must have been watching him like a hawk, rasped out, "Sure that match is out, Pelham?"

George glanced up in offended surprise and looked around, reached over and ground out the pin-point of flame creeping along the match. "Sorry," he said over his shoulder.

"Just remember that, will you?" Joe said shortly. "It's against the rules to start a forest fire in the Park."

"Just go to the devil, will you?" George replied calmly, but very much under his breath. He turned back to me.

"—After Steve was killed we found he'd literally hounded the poor guy out of the office."

"What for?" I demanded. There was no reason why I should have been angry, but I was. Not at Steve Grant for hounding the poor guy out of the office, but at George for saying so.

"I guess maybe he knew too much," he said casually. "We tried to find him to make it up to him, but he'd moved. You know how it is in New York."

I tried to sound as casual. After all, Steve Grant was nothing to me. "—What do you mean, he knew too much?"

"We never went into it," George said. "Cecily's father quashed it before it got around. There was something funny about a check. Steve had made it good, all right, I'll say that for him. Anyway, the customer was a zany old gal. She wouldn't have prosecuted. But it did throw a lot of light on things. I thought Johnny'd got a raw deal. He was a good man."

He started to toss his cigarette out into the grass, remembered and dug up half a dozen harebells and blue gentians with his heel, dropped it in the hole and kicked the dirt and mangled flowers over it.

"But I always thought he wasn't himself after he got back," he said tolerantly. "He wasn't really responsible for what he did."

The cook banged on the bottom of his frying pan, George leaped up. "I'm starved! Where are my fish? Oh boy, look at 'em!"

For some reason the brown luscious strips, hot and crisp at the edges and soft pink inside, didn't taste as good as they should have done. I kept thinking of the two divergent pictures I'd got of this person Steven Grant. It seemed clear to me that Mrs. Chapman had never heard the story of the check and the man Johnny Brice that George had just told me so casually. I doubted very much if anyone would have dared so much as try to tell it to her. But Cecily was different. The suggestion of suicide could hardly account for the scene her grandmother had described in the library that evening. In the long hours of the months that followed his death she must have faced that dark probability from time to time herself, knowing as only she did what had happened before he left her to go crashing to his death.

But the story George had told me would be more than enough, I thought, to rouse her passionate fury against the man who told it to her, and her own father, who must have corroborated it.

And she could disbelieve George, but she could not disbelieve her own father. No matter how fiercely she'd denied it, she must have come to some kind of terms with it, to have allowed George to come to see her again. But never to complete acceptance. That was the only thing that could explain the question that seemed to me to lie behind her grave amber-flecked eyes. It was a conflict that was never lulled to final rest, a conflict between belief and doubt, between reason and emotion, evidence and instinct. It seemed to me almost as if the ghost of a dead man was sitting there just then, at the camp fire with us.

A pale wraith of smoke curled up and eddied softly out across the lake. The lonely howl of a coyote came eerily back over the darkening water. Steve Grant was dead, but alive for that moment in the consciousness of three people in this vast wilderness two thousand miles from where he'd lived and moved and . . . died. And perhaps still more poignantly and intensely alive for a fourth. I glanced at Cecily. She'd suddenly put down her plate and got to her feet. She turned and walked quickly down to the lake. Her grandmother watched her silently for a moment. Then she said, "If you're through, George, I guess we can clean up."

Even the next morning as we crossed the Continental

Divide on Two Ocean Plateau, I couldn't get Steve Grant entirely out of my mind.

Coming down the steep tortuous wooded trail along Lynx Creek, with George (and me too) keeping a cautious eye out for grizzly bears, I couldn't help wondering about him. I knew now that Cecily had been thinking about him too. Her grandmother had said, quite unexpectedly, as she and I came back from walking a little way along the lake shore before breakfast, "I expect maybe I'm being a little hard on Cecily. We camped here last when Steve was with us. He was great fun to have along. He loved the woods."

I'd forgot him, however, as the trail flattened out across the full rushing channel of Lynx Creek, and a cow moose with her big-nosed calf fled across the marsh into the low willows. Three antlered elk slipped quietly across our path into the woods as we came into sight of the Yellowstone River through the trees. The trail turned left, and in front of us lay a broad meadow, green-gold under the sparkling sapphire sky. Far across it, beyond the dark rim of pines, rose the vast dun-colored fortress of The Trident. We forded the swift river into the open valley. The trail, marked with fresh-cut lodgepole pines, meandered through grass thick with gentians, blue and fringed, and yellow cinquefoil and paintbrush —a tapestry of gold and red and blue woven with wild flowers I'd never seen or heard of before.

We stopped at Thorofare Creek, where the trail wound on ahead to the Ranger Station, tucked away hidden in the pines at the foot of the mountains. Another trail crossed it on the other side of the creek, going south to the Teton Forest and north to Yellowstone proper.

After lunch George got up.

"I think I'll go to the Ranger Station and register for us," he said easily. "I don't think they ought to seal our guns. What if we meet a grizzly?"

"You turn sharply left and climb the nearest tree," Mrs. Chapman said smoothly. "You'll be surprised how easy it is."

George looked skeptical. He turned to Joe Anders.

"I'll take your papers, Anders," he said. "You can give me your gun too."

"Thanks," Joe said shortly. "I'll go myself. I've got to check up on our fire permit."

Bill, who'd planned all the way down the mountain to go with Joe, put his foot in his stirrup.

"I'll go along anyway," George said. "They won't want to

be unreasonable. Anyway, I know a lot of people in Washington."

Joe Anders shot him a swift hostile glance and swung up into his saddle. I saw Bill take his foot out of the stirrup and drop his reins on the ground. Joe looked back, half-way across the creek. "Coming, Bill?"

"I'll stay and help pack," Bill said, with a nonchalance that failed to deceive anybody. And because I knew how much he'd planned on seeing a Ranger in a Ranger Station, I was definitely disturbed. He'd never before in his life been able to conduct a feud for more than two consecutive hours. I hadn't realized up to then just how much my son didn't like George Pelham.

He and Joe must have been gone three-quarters of an hour before we saw them coming back again across the meadow.

"I guess Pelham doesn't know the right people in Washington," Joe said with a sardonic flicker as we joined them on the other side of the creek. "Anyhow, both guns are sealed."

I looked at George. He was definitely not amused. In fact he was extremely upset. The skin around his lips was a curious grey, and his eyes had the most extraordinary look in them that I've ever seen. It couldn't have been fear, I thought —except that that was just what it looked like. With all his faults I should never have thought of him as being timid. It was almost incredible. He turned abruptly to Mrs. Chapman.

"I don't think it's safe," he said stubbornly. "The fire guard said we might very easily meet bears. I think we ought to go back. Nobody wants to see the geysers anyway. Why don't we just go across the meadow to Bridger Lake and spend a couple of days fishing?"

There was the tiniest fraction of silence before Mrs. Chapman spoke.

"Because Grace and Bill are meeting some friends at the lake tomorrow evening," she said flatly. "If you don't care to come, you can camp at Bridger Lake and we'll pick you up on Friday on our way back. The rest of us are going on."

George hesitated. Then he shrugged. "Oh, all right," he said.

He took his gun out of his pocket and looked down at it. The trigger was held by thin wires and sealed with two little pellets of lead—the sort that stores fasten price tags on expensive furs with, so women can't wear them and return them two days later. He slipped it back into his pocket.

"I hope you won't be sorry," he said grimly. "Let's go."

Joe Anders reached out to take the lead line from Bill. "You didn't miss much," he said. "Only the fire guard was there."

The sun was just going down when we crossed Cabin Creek a half mile or so from where we were to spend the night beside the Yellowstone River. We'd seen elk and moose and woodchucks and squirrels, and a doe with two spotted fawns, but we hadn't seen so much as even a track of a bear. Suddenly as the trail wound left through the woods we came upon a tiny log cabin set inside a rail fence in a lonely little clearing jutting out from the side of the hill. The windows were tightly shuttered and barred. Then as we came into the corral yard we saw one with the shutter raised and propped open, and the door was standing open too, giving it suddenly a friendly inhabited air in an uninhabited wilderness. Long slanting streaks of sunlight through the trees lighted up the dim interior. I could see a range and a woodbox full of wood and a cupboard against the wall, and a cot stacked with folded bedding in the middle of the floor. Outside the door was a big pile of freshly cut wood with a bucksaw leaning against it.

"I guess the Ranger's been here," Joe Anders said. "The fire guard said he was out this way repairing the telephone line. This is another snowshoe cabin. They keep 'em stocked with thirty days' rations to use in winter when they're patrolling the area on skis."

He didn't get off his horse. "We'll come back and have a look later, Bill."

We went through the corral fence and down the steep path across the little creek, and wound out into the meadow on the bank of the wide river bed. And there, looking down on the sandy edge, we did see a bear track—a broad soft pad clearly defined in the sand.

I glanced at George. He was still standing looking down at it minutes after the rest of us had moved away, Joe and Cecily and Bill and the cook to unpack and unsaddle for the night, me to limber up my congealed muscles. I was a little distance from the others and off to one side, out of the line of George's vision. It was rather amusing, watching his concentrated scrutiny of that pad in the sand. Or it was for a moment—until I saw him reach in his pocket, slip out his gun and look at it a long time.

He glanced over his shoulder up toward the little cabin hidden in the pines. His eyes travelling back rested for a moment on Joe Anders's lean figure. Then quite suddenly he reached in his pocket again, took out a knife and opened it. I didn't see him cut the wires, but I saw something drop on the ground in front of him, and saw him grind it sharply into the ground with his heel. He hadn't looked my way at all, up to then, and when he did I was busily engaged watching a frog in the grass. I could feel his eyes boring through me for an instant. Then he moved back toward the others.

"What can I do?" he inquired amiably.

It was the first time, so far as I could recall, that he'd ever offered his services. Nobody seemed particularly impressed. After a moment of just standing, he wandered off up the river, while the others took the horses down the meadow to turn them out to pasture. I could hear the tinkle of the lead horse's bell and the low disappearing thud of their hoofs behind the willows, mingling softly with the wilderness undertones of whispering pine and singing water.

It should have been very pleasant there, just then, at the end of the long day, but it wasn't, some way. I had, for some reason I couldn't possibly explain, a chill sense of impending danger that made all of it suddenly seem unbearably isolated and lonely and inimical. I moved around gathering up wood for the fire, trying to shake it off. After all, I kept telling myself, nothing very awful could happen to us, even if George Pelham did meet a bear and shoot it. If he went to jail in spite of his friends in Washington, that was definitely his problem, not mine. But I couldn't shake it off. The cook obviously thought so little of my efforts at wood-gathering that I quit after my second armful. He and Mrs. Chapman stopped talking so abruptly both times I came back to them that I wandered off too, in the opposite direction to that George had taken.

Perhaps I took the trail up to the snowshoe cabin unconsciously, because it represented a tangible human toehold in an empty wilderness. I'm not sure. I do know that my heart jumped as I raised my head to listen. Suddenly out of the woods in front of me came the clop-clop of a horse's hoofs, and a magnificent baritone voice singing lustily at the top of its lungs:

"Heigh-ho, heigh-ho, home from work we go!"

Whether I distinguished the words at first I don't know, but in a minute I did—and there was such sheer joy of being alive in them, and in the warm voice bellowing them out, that I found myself hurrying along up the trail, completely forgetting that my knees were stiff and that I was tired and hungry.

I came to the clear brook at the foot of the steep bank up to the cabin yard, and stopped, listening. I could hear the horse stamping, and a cheerful voice saying, "Whoa, Molly. Just a minute, girl! There you are, old lady. How about another drink?"

The mare, recognizing the presence of other horses, I suppose, whinnied long and tremulously. An answering whinny came up from the meadow.

"We've got company tonight," I heard the Ranger say. "We'll call after supper."

It was a pleasant educated voice, boyish but deep and full-timbered as a man's. I could hear the creak of leather and the clank of metal on the corral fence, and then his quick steps across the yard, suddenly sharper as he reached the concrete doorsteps. Then they stopped, abruptly.

I jumped across the little brook and ran up the steep path. Through the pine rail fence I saw him standing, almost filling the cabin door, his back to me, one foot a little forward, every muscle taut and rigid as if he'd suddenly turned to stone half-way across the threshold. He was over six feet, I'd say, and his shoulders under the drab gabardine shirt were straight and muscular. He had on olive green trousers tucked in heavy black oiled boots. In one hand he carried a sheathed double-bitted axe, in the other a thick coil of wire and the kind of leather harness you see on men up telephone poles. And he didn't move. He just stood, stock-still in the door.

I stood stock-still too. There was something so galvanized, so dynamic, in every tense fibre of the man's body that I was just frozen in my tracks. He hadn't, obviously, heard me scrambling up the bank. Every faculty and nerve was concentrated on something beyond him through the cabin door —something that had shocked him into absolute rigidity. Then, abruptly and completely disembodied, as if a radio had been turned on in an empty room, came George Pelham's cool Eastern voice.

"Hello . . . Steve. I thought it was going to be you. The fire guard said the Ranger was out—and he showed us some snapshots of a man he called Sam Graham——"

My hand reached out and caught hold of the corral fence, and clung to it, completely dissociated from the rest of my nerveless body. I just stood there, totally appalled, too dumfounded and too shattered to move or breathe.

22

"—So you weren't killed after all, were you? I used to wonder about that. Remember the movie we saw in Trenton the night I had the flat?"

The tiny log cabin, the corral yard, the dark pines that hemmed them in, swirled dizzily in a confused blur in my mind, around the lean erect figure of the Ranger, motionless and unflinching in the doorway.

Steve Grant, dead three years, was alive and strong, facing George Pelham across the threshold of a cabin door in a desolate wilderness where no one ever came. And George had known, ever since he left the Ranger Station at Thorofare, that he was somewhere there. His face grey around the lips, his eyes alive with something I hadn't quite dared call fear, flashed back into my mind. The grizzly then, from that moment, had been a flimsy pretext to avoid just this. I could hear his voice saying to Mrs. Chapman, "I hope you won't be sorry . . ."

Then I heard it again, cool and arrogant, speaking to the man there in the door, whose name was supposed to be Sam Graham:

"Cecily and Mrs. Chapman are down below . . . just in case——"

So suddenly that I hardly realized what was happening, the Ranger strode forward. I stood, staring at the blank closed door filling the space where he'd been, at his axe upright against the woodpile, his telephone gear in a heap on the step beside it. I stood there for a long moment, my lips quite dry, my feet cold as blocks of ice. Then I turned and slipped as noiselessly as I could down the bank, across the brook and along the trail into the open. It was like moving in a nightmare, trying to escape from some shattering blow that would send everything crashing down around my head. Only it wasn't my head I was thinking of. It was Cecily Chapman—and her grandmother too. I could hear her saying, "He was the finest human being I ever knew or ever hope to know . . ." But it was Cecily who mattered—Cecily and years of faith and poignant devotion.

3

I stopped abruptly. Far across the meadow I could see her, a bright spot of plaid and gold and blue in the long low fingers of light from the setting sun. She and Joe Anders and Bill were trooping back from turning out the horses. It seemed so incredible and fantastic that she should be so close to the one clear reality her life had ever known and not know it, not some way sense it.

She saw me first and waved her red bandanna. Bill and Joe waved too, and I waved back, hardly conscious of what I was doing. It was all too awful.

"Steve Grant isn't dead. He's alive. He's not dead." It kept throbbing a ghastly tattoo in the pulse of my throat. "Steve Grant couldn't do anything ungallant, or dishonorable, or disloyal." Mrs. Chapman's words, spoken with so much quiet conviction, came back too. But they were suddenly and cruelly disproved. He had allowed them to believe he was dead. He'd run off, leaving Cecily so shocked and shattered it had taken her three years to regain—her grandmother had said—something of her old vivid quicksilver quality again.

And I could hear her saying: "And I don't want anything ever to destroy it again." It was George she was thinking of, but George wasn't Cecily's danger now. What would happen to her when she knew Steve Grant had just calmly walked out and left her, changed his name and hidden himself out in the wilderness, letting them think he was dead? If that wasn't ungallant, and dishonorable, and disloyal, then words no longer had any meaning.

I turned back abruptly. One thing seemed perfectly clear and urgent to me just then. Steve Grant had got to stay dead as far as Cecily could ever know. I had to see George at once —he couldn't be allowed to tell her.

But it was too late then. Cecily came running across the meadow, Bill beside her.

"Was that the Ranger we heard?" he shouted.

I stopped and turned around, moistened my lips and brushed my hair off my forehead, and tried to compose what must have been distorted features. I didn't succeed very well, because Cecily stopped short as she came up.

"Grace—what *is* the matter? You look as if you'd seen a ghost!"

"Don't be silly," I said. My voice sounded sharper than I'd meant it to. "I'm just tired, I guess."

I had seen a ghost . . . but that's the last thing in the world I wanted her to know.

"You'd better go sit down," she said. "Bill and I are going up to see the Lone Ranger."

"No!" I thought desperately; *"no!"* and I tried hopelessly to think of some casual natural way I could stop them.

Bill was already on his way. "Come on, Cecily!" he shouted back impatiently. She started after him. I stood there helplessly, my brain completely paralyzed. Just then from the camp fire on the river bank came the bang-clang of an iron spoon on the bottom of a frying pan, and the cook's squeaky voice: "Soup! Soo-oop! Come and get it!"

My heart missed a beat as my son stopped short in his tracks and turned around, his face shining.

"Supper's ready!" he shouted. "Come on, Cess—let's eat! Let the Lone Ranger wait!"

He grabbed her hand and they dashed back past me down the trail, laughing and shouting to the cook; I thought for a moment that if I didn't sit down I'd fall down. My knees were shaking like aspen leaves. But there wasn't any place to sit, so I didn't. I walked slowly back to the camp.

Mrs. Chapman was sitting cross-legged by the fire. Cecily and Bill were helping the cook ladle soup out of the smoky-bottomed pot. Cecily looked around.

"Where's George?"

She handed me a tin cup full of thick steaming black bean soup.

I shook my head. "I wouldn't know," I said.

"Out checking up on bears, probably." Her grandmother looked up without concern. "I wish he'd meet one, myself. Sit down, Grace. You look half dead."

I sat down.

"I wonder where he is?" Cecily insisted. "This isn't like him at all."

She put her cupped hands to her face and called "George! George! Food, George!"

Her voice, clear in its higher registers, went up toward the pine-mantled hills and echoed back across the meadow. Something tightened in the pit of my stomach as suddenly, for some reason I can't explain unless it was the sound of her voice, calling clear and sweet through the twilight afterglow, I felt passionately, poignantly sorry for Steven Grant. Whatever he'd done and for whatever reason, Cecily's voice, reaching him up there in the lonely clearing in the pines, calling another man, must be tearing his heart almost out of him.

Abruptly out of the distance came George's "Halloo —coming!" and we saw him swinging down the trail out of the woods. I knew that Steve Grant had heard her voice, then. I could almost see him up there in front of the tiny snowshoe cabin, leaning against the rail fence, looking down, thinking . . . no one could know what, of course. But I'd heard his voice. I'd heard a shrewd hard-bitten old woman, her eyes and her voice suddenly very tender, talk about him beside a mountain lake in the evening . . . and I knew he couldn't help but be going through some kind of very special hell. And instantly at that moment all my doubts and misgivings about Steve Grant faded quietly away, and left in their place, as sharp as if a drop of acid had fallen there, a piercing suspicion of George Pelham.

Why had he unsealed his gun before he went up to see his former friend? Why had his face been so strained and grey around the lips after he'd seen Steve Grant's picture in the Ranger Station at Thorofare, and knew he was somewhere there along the trail to Cabin Creek? It wasn't only that he wanted to save Cecily—I could have sworn to that. He'd been willing enough for her to risk her neck on the palomino to save his. I knew instantly, as well as if he'd told me himself, that he had some other reason for being afraid of Steve Grant, of wanting to see him alone before anyone else could see him.

He came striding blithely up to the camp fire.

"Sorry I'm late," he said.

Through the fragrant veil of smoke I saw his face with a kind of momentary shock that startled me so I had to put down my soup to keep from spilling it. All the grim concentration of the afternoon was wiped out as thoroughly as if it had never existed. In its place was a complete confidence that was almost like triumph. Whatever had happened behind the closed door of the snowshoe cabin had happened exactly the way George Pelham had wanted it to happen. That much was clearer than the waning moon coming up in the eastern sky.

He took his cup of soup and sat down beside Cecily on the other side of the fire. There was something so proprietary about the way he did it, crowding Bill aside a little, that I saw Mrs. Chapman's eyes sharpen with apprehension. She glanced at her granddaughter, her square jaw hardening. Cecily, unconscious of any of it, looked up with a smile.

"Did you find a bear?"

George laughed.

"I found the Ranger."

Cecily looked down into the fire, her eyes soft, her lips parted a little. "That was him singing, wasn't it?—It sounded like . . . someone I used to know."

My heart stood still. The soup cup in George's hand was motionless for a second as he looked at her in the firelight. Mrs. Chapman's voice broke a tension that only he and I were aware of.

"Why didn't you ask him to come down and have supper with us?" she demanded.

"I did," George said calmly. "He said he was too busy."

Joe Anders frowned.

"It's funny he didn't come down and have a look at our permit," he said. He looked at George, a skeptical flicker in his shrewd outdoor eyes. "I guess I'll go up and have a look-see."

He put down his plate and got to his feet. George shrugged his shoulders and raised his cup to his lips.

Joe stood looking down at him, frowning, not quite sure, apparently, what it was all about. "He didn't tell you you could unseal your gun, did he?" he asked quietly.

"As a matter of fact, he did."

George set his plate down, took his gun out of his pocket and held it out coolly.

"He unsealed it for me, if you'd like to know it."

I caught my breath. There's something pretty appalling about a person telling a plain, deliberate falsehood. I looked at Joe. His lean brown face had hardened, his eyes fixed directly on George were narrowed.

"I think you're lying," he said quietly.

George flushed, his body stiffened.

"Shut up, both of you," Mrs. Chapman said sharply. "Sit down, Joe. George, you stay where you are."

George shrugged. "You can apologize later, Anders," he said calmly.

"Stop it, Joe!" Mrs. Chapman's voice was icy. "I don't want this referred to again on this trip. And I'll take that gun, George. Give it to me at once."

George handed her the gun without a murmur and went coolly on with his supper. Joe Anders sat down again, the muscles in his cheeks standing out in tense wire ridges, his eyes fixed grimly on the fire.

I looked at George. His face was in the shadow of Cecily's head, but as she bent forward to put an orange peel into the fire, I saw it plainly for an instant. He was smiling a faint curious smile that was like the sudden impact of a blow. I put down my plate. It seems utterly crazy now to say that it wasn't until that instant that the necessary corollary of Steve Grant's being alive struck me, but it's quite true. The shock of seeing him, the fear of the devastating effect it might have on Cecily, had completely blinded me to everything else. That smile on George's face shot it into my awareness like a rocket into the night.

Steve Grant was alive—a ranger out in the wilderness, more than two thousand miles from the house he'd left one Sunday night three years before. Less than two hundred yards separated him this moment from the girl who'd stood stanchly by him through his illness, and whose grandmother had found her in a heap of passionate tears on the floor when he'd gone. Cecily's face and her wide-set amber eyes as clear as stars, so unconscious that the man she'd loved was just up there in the cabin yard, was all I'd thought of till now. But— if it wasn't Steve Grant's body in the burned twisted car . . . whose was it? Who had Steve Grant left, to be found and buried and grieved for, in his place?

And George Pelham was thinking of that too. In fact—it followed instantly in my mind—he must have thought of it many times before, if he'd spoken the truth up there in the cabin. "So you weren't killed after all, were you? I've often wondered about that." If he had wondered about it, he must have gone further, he couldn't have stopped just there. And where—I wondered myself—would he stop now? Steven Grant for better or for worse was at George Pelham's mercy; and George Pelham's mercy would suit George Pelham's interest, wherever it lay. I knew that was what he was thinking of now, sitting quietly there in the shadows behind Cecily, smiling faintly to himself.

Joe Anders tossed the remnants from his tin plate into the fire and handed it to the cook. He got deliberately to his feet.

"I'm going to see the Ranger, Mrs. Chapman," he said shortly. "Something around here looks screwy to me. I think I'll just check up. Want to come along, Bill?"

Bill was on his feet in an instant, his face lighted up with joy. "You bet!" he exclaimed. "Come on, Cecily—I'll beat you to the woods!"

My heart gave a sharp downward lunge. Cecily laughed gaily. Then she was up like a flash and the two of them streaked off like a pair of young colts up the bank and along the trail, shirt tails flying. George, lighting a cigarette, held the match in his fingers until it burned almost to the tip, dropped it and put his heel on it, his face shuttered and enigmatic. Joe Anders glanced around at me. "Would you like to come, Mrs. Latham?"

I got up. "I'd . . . like to," I said.

"How about you, Mrs. Chapman?"

She shook her head. "I'll stay here."

George hadn't stirred. He just sat there, blowing long feathers of smoke from his nostrils, watching them rise and mingle with the pale sweet smoke from the pine fire.

Joe and I walked quickly along the narrow trail. The luminous disc of the moon was deepening as the last vestige of daylight faded into night. It seemed very cold, all of a sudden, and Cecily and Bill, puffing and laughing where they'd stopped for breath at the edge of the dark woods, sounded strident and unreal, as if they had no right to be laughing here.

If I could only stop her, some way, I thought helplessly. If there was only something I could do to keep her from leaping lightly across the little brook and running up that last short stretch into the cabin yard. But there wasn't. There was nothing I could do. Perhaps Fate itself had written this dark chapter long before she was born, and there was no power that could stop it now until its bitter end was read.

Joe and I walked along in silence. Cecily and Bill waited until we were almost to them, and dashed off again. I quickened my pace. The trail through the pine trees was getting darker. The golden ball of light from Joe's electric flash bounced along at my feet. I heard Bill shout "Jump, Cecily!" and heard the splash of water. I was almost running myself. Then I could see their two slim figures reach the top of the steep bank across the brook, and the corral fence. I jumped across the brook and ran up.

Cecily and Bill were in the cabin yard. The bleached antlers of an elk stood out white and ghostly at the end of the low rooftree. The saw by the woodpile was gone, the zinc-covered door was shut and heavily padlocked. A pale circle of oats lay on the ground where Molly had been tethered to the fence. Steve Grant was gone. There was nothing but silence in the lonely little clearing in the woods.

4

My khaki silk-lined sleeping bag was like a straight jacket that night. I lay there looking up at the vast frosty white silence of the heavens, trying to reconcile what seemed humanly irreconcilable, and failing that, trying to put it all out of my mind, and succeeding at nothing. The voice I'd heard in the cabin yard, the man Mrs. Chapman had talked about—neither of them fitted the man passing as Sam Graham, who'd slipped off from a burning car by a roadside leaving another man dead in his place, or the man who'd slipped away again this night, alone into the wilderness.

A pale wreath of smoke wound up from the camp fire still burning on the river bank, and floated up into the dark pine tops massed against the hill side. Somewhere along the lonely trail Steve Grant would be making his solitary way, Cecily's voice still calling in his ears. She was sitting now, long after all the rest of us had turned in for the night, with George Pelham beside the small camp fire. Their voices came to me in fitful splashes mixed with pine smoke by the eddying breeze, George's blurred but very urgent, Cecily's clear and carrying.

Heaven knows I've eavesdropped enough in my left-handed association with my friends Colonel Primrose and Sergeant Buck, but always with at least apparent justification. This had none except plain unadulterated curiosity, and the fact that unless I put my head down in my sleeping bag and smothered to death I couldn't possibly avoid it.

Cecily's light, obviously parrying rejoinder to something I hadn't heard reached my ears. "—You promised not to bring that up again until we were back in New York. Remember?"

"But I can't wait that long, Cecily. You know I love, and I want you, and I've waited for years because you're worth waiting a lifetime for. But it can't go on forever, Cecily. Can't you tell me now? Steve's never coming back. You can't go on year after year eating your heart out. I know you'll never care as much for me as you did for him, but if we had a home and children to take his place, you'd forget it quicker."

"I suppose I would," Cecily said slowly. Then she said after a long time, "There isn't anybody else I'd marry, George. It's just that . . . I don't feel like marrying . . . at all. And maybe you and father were right in telling me what you did about Steve, but . . . well, I'd decided to marry you before that, because you understood about Steve—but . . . after that I couldn't tell. It did something funny to me . . . whether it was true or not.—And I've never believed it, not in my heart. Steve wasn't that kind."

"But if you knew he was? You could see old Mrs. Stuyvesant. I've told you what she said. 'I've gambled too, and lost. He gambled and did very well. I'm glad to have loaned him the money, even if I didn't know it. I've got it back, and I don't want to be bothered any more.' She was swell about it."

"It doesn't sound like Steve," Cecily said quietly. "It just doesn't."

There was a long silence. I held my breath. Would he tell her now that Steve Grant was alive, that he'd been up there this evening, just behind the dark fringe of pines, knowing how close he was to her? Perhaps he thought the balance was too delicate, that Cecily's loyalty to Steve would be great enough to surmount even that. All he said was, "It's getting late. You ought to be in bed."

He got to his feet and held his hand down to help her up. "—Maybe some day you'll see it differently."

She stood there looking up at him, her hair glowing in the powdered moonlight with the soft patina of antique silver gilt.

"I'm sorry, George," she said gently. "I wish I didn't feel the way I do. But I do."

He lifted her hand and held it for a moment against his lips.

"Run along to bed, little girl. I'll put the fire out."

I heard her unzip the side of her sleeping bag and crawl in, and zip it up again. It was a long time, it seemed to me, before I heard her soft breath rise and fall evenly and I knew she was asleep. It was a long time after that that George Pelham got up again from beside the fire. What decision he'd come to I couldn't know. That he'd come to one I could tell from the sharp decisive way he trod out the last live embers before he went to the other side of the tent to his bed.

Waiting the next morning at the Southeast Arm of Yellowstone Lake for the boat to pick us up, I still couldn't sort out the business of Steve Grant and the night before so that it made any possible sense. Here in the intense clarity of another scene, the nine miles we'd come from the locked and shuttered snowshoe cabin in the pines seemed like twice that many years stretching back into a crazy fantastic dream.

In front of us the long sunlit pier reached out into the calm blue water. A faint mauve haze softened the rounding peaks of the Absarokas, rimming the horizon of a cloudless sky as pale and clear as a flax blossom. A pair of trumpeter swans in liquid motion sailed above the sapphire bay. I looked down at Cecily, sitting at the end of the pier with George and Bill, her bright head tilted back, her brown hands clasping her slim knees in their rough blue jeans. They were watching three great satin-sleek bull moose, their antlers bent forward, browsing in the marshy willows where the river widens into the lake a little way back along the curving wooded line of the shore. It didn't seem real or possible that this girl, as sparkling and uninvolved just then as the sun-light dancing on the crystal surface of the water, could be the focal point of impending tragedy.

Mrs. Chapman was sitting by me on the rough-hewn steps of the storage cabin at the land end of the pier. "You don't know what a relief it was to me to see the rear end of Joe Anders and the pack string," she said. "They'll go back to the cabin and around the side of the lake, and meet us at the other end. It'll take them two days, and by that time Joe'll have cooled off—I hope. Joe's a very special person. He was in the Park Service after he finished the University of Wyoming. I met him here five years ago and persuaded him to come to Cinnabar. He's managed it for me ever since. I couldn't get along without Joe."

She glanced down at the end of the pier, a sardonic flicker lighting her eyes.

"I could get along without George very nicely, but I wouldn't want them to hang Joe for it."

The flicker in her eyes faded. "You know, the more I see of George Pelham, the more I don't want Cecily to marry him. In fact, there's nothing I wouldn't do to keep her from it, Grace—*nothing*."

I didn't look at her, but I knew that what was in that square old iron jaw matched the grim determination in her brusque speech.

"How did he ever happen to get in the running?" I asked. "Isn't he older than most of her friends?"

"He's thirty-three. He got in the running because he was Steve Grant's best friend in Cecily's father's office."

I looked at her. Friendship hadn't been the keynote of the scene in the cabin the night before, or the conversation I'd had with George at Mariposa. "A fellow I knew," he called Steve then; and last night he'd unsealed a gun and taken it with him to their meeting.

"He stood by like an older brother when Steve was away that year—at least that's what Steve and Cecily thought. I didn't. I tried to put a stop to it even then. But after Steve died, he was the only tangible link Cecily had left with him. I tried every way I could to discourage it, especially after he'd told her father he wanted to marry her.—I may do George an injustice, and I have no reason to say this except an old woman's intuition . . . but I think George, with all his breeding and charm, could be as ruthless and vindictive as an Indian, if he chose."

A cold shiver went down my spine. I thought so too.

"It sounds fanciful, and I'm not much given to fancy," Mrs. Chapman went on grimly. "But I've had a feeling all summer that something's going to blow up that's going to settle all this—one way or the other. I've been afraid to move, for fear something I'd do would bring it on, and either throw her into his arms or put him out of her life forever. If I could be sure it would be the latter I'd welcome it. But I'm not. No one was ever born who could predict the way Cecily's going to react. I certainly wouldn't try it, and I know her better than anyone else. I've raised her from a baby. She's dearer to me than any child of my own ever was."

For a long moment I sat there, biting my tongue to keep from blurting out the whole story of Steven Grant. Then it flashed into my mind that if I did, I'd probably be the agent who'd bring on the crisis that Mrs. Chapman was waiting for, and dreading—and it was a responsibility that I had no right or business to assume. Only my uneasy distrust of George Pelham, the part he'd played and his barely concealed triumph, made me waver a little.

I looked down at them again. Bill had taken out his knife, and the three of them were playing mumbly-peg on the rough pine timbers of the pier, the imminent hazard of the knife going through a crack into the deep water adding breathless shrieking excitement to the game. Heaven knows George looked harmless enough just then. It occurred to me that nothing he could ever do to Cecily could hurt as much as the knowledge that Steve Grant had deliberately and wilfully deceived her. And somehow—I realized just then—I'd made up my mind, in the course of our ride in from Cabin Creek that morning, that he would never tell her. It would be stupid, and whatever George Pelham was, he wasn't stupid. It seemed to me he must at least recognize where his own interest lay. Even he would have to know that some wounds never heal, and if you destroy what you're trying to get before you get it, there's not much satisfaction in having it.

Suddenly over the water we heard the hum of a motor. The game on the pier came to a hilarious end, the knife still on deck. They jumped up, waving to the motor-boat pilot sounding a greeting on his horn, the bow of his trim gleaming craft cutting two long white feathers of spray through the sapphire blue surface of the water. In another moment he swung deftly alongside the pier, jumped out, his face beaming, shook hands with Cecily and bounded up the pier to shake hands with Mrs. Chapman.

"Glad to see you back, Mrs. Chapman. How's everything at Cinnabar? Did you see a ranger coming along? We're supposed to take him back with us if he was here."

"He had to go back to the Station," George called over his shoulder. "I was talking to him last night."

"Okay then, if you're ready. Here—put these on."

The pilot pulled a lot of green oilskin sou-westers out of the boat and helped Mrs. Chapman on with one of them. I was the only one who wasn't ready. It took me a full minute to recover from the fact that before he knew who we were, Steve Grant had planned to finish the journey from Cabin Creek to Lake Junction with us. What if George hadn't intercepted him, I thought—and we'd all met there on the pier? What a quaint scene that would have been!

I was still thinking about it as we shot out of the little bay through the channel and passed The Promontory into the open lake. Not even the swarm of pelicans, standing sagely about like a congress of yellow-beaked philosophers, their chins on their snowy shirt-fronts, as we swerved left to have a look at the tiny pair of islands where they breed in undisturbed solitude, took it entirely out of my mind. I glanced back at George. He and Cecily were ducked down together in the narrow rear seat, laughing merrily as each sharp turn of the boat practically inundated them with spray, having a wonderful time.

I'd had no notion that Yellowstone Lake was as enormous as it was, even if I had read somewhere that it's the second largest body of water of its altitude in the world. The channel of the secluded bay had faded far behind us before we neared the other side and I got my first glimpse of the dazzling white columns and long yellow wings of the Lake Hotel. I rather wish now that it had been my last. Certainly the almost dizzy feeling of relief that I had when I climbed up on the wharf and looked back at the narrow passage between the low rounded peaks of the Absaroka Range and the pine-wooded slopes of the Red Mountain was premature to say the least. It was like escaping from a sputtering popping string of firecrackers and sitting down to relax on a keg of dynamite with the detonator all set.

But at that moment, looking up at the lofty dignity of the pseudo-Georgian pile—if anything stretching out endlessly like a mammoth train of palatial yellow cars can be called a pile—it seemed to me we had escaped very real tragedy indeed.

We were certainly definitely back in civilization. Cars crowded the high brow of the bank. A government launch pulled tediously off from the Fisheries dock lined with people. Half a dozen boatloads of fishermen pushed off from our dock, gaping at our extraordinary regalia. A string of yellow buses swung up the Loop road and round the drive up to the white-columned portico of the hotel. A pleasant shining-faced youngster in a green uniform came dashing across the road to meet us.

"Your car's here with your things, Mrs. Chapman," he said cheerfully. "We thought you'd get here before the dudes flocked in." He turned to me.

"Are you Mrs. Latham? Colonel Primrose said if you came before he got back, to tell you he had to go down to Government headquarters, and he'd be back around five.—I guess a bath and change your clothes is what you all want before you have any company."

It mightn't have been tactful, but it was certainly true. The dudes crowding into the spacious sun-splashed lounge with its tubs of oleanders and gorgeous curtains blocked with brilliant wildflowers and cool gaily upholstered wicker furniture, stared at us goggle-eyed. Suddenly out of the long line in front of the desk an astonished voice sounded.

"*George!* My God, look at him, May!"

A large blond man of about fifty, in a perfectly-tailored grey chalk-striped flannel suit and brown-and-white shoes, disengaged himself from the line and came over to us, his hand out.

"Bless me!" he said heartily. "Is it a Wild West Show? Hello, Cecily. Did they let him wear that dude rig at Cinnabar? How d'ye do, Mrs. Chapman?"

George turned—a little stiffly, I thought—to me.

"Grace, this is my brother-in-law. Mr. Ridley—Mrs. Latham. And this is Bill Latham."

He bent down and kissed the slight, rather meek, grey-haired little woman who'd come in Alexander Ridley's cordial swell.

"Hello, May. How did you people get out here? You've met Mrs. Chapman and Cecily—and this is Mrs. Latham, and Bill Latham. This is my sister, Grace."

I hope I didn't say, "Oh, really?" It was on the tip of my tongue, certainly. How anybody as gentle and indefinite and old could be George's sister was a mystery to me.

"Alexander thought it would be nice if we came," she said. "We were in San Francisco at the Fair, and it didn't cost anything extra to be routed this way. It's very interesting. Old Faithful spouted just as our bus drove up yesterday, and just as it left again today."

Mr. Alexander Ridley had taken complete charge of Cecily. His wife followed him with anxious tired eyes. They'd gone over to look out of the broad bay windows at the shimmering blue water of the lake. "Finest view I've seen anywhere," Mr. Ridley's voice came back heartily. "Fine trip —fine park. Wouldn't have missed it for worlds."

"Is your daughter with you?" Mrs. Chapman asked.

"She's in another bus," Mrs. Ridley said. "Alexander likes her to be with young people."

Bill and I strolled off to look around . . . and came, then and there, without the slightest warning and with awful suddenness, face to face with a large square granite figure wedged in a rose-upholstered wicker chair at least five sizes too small for him. As Sergeant Phineas T. Buck's eyes caught mine, his newspaper halted midway to his knees. He stared at me fishy-eyed, his stony fissured visage slowly turning the color of tarnished brass. Then he jerked himself up, prying himself loose from the protesting fibre, and got to his feet, his cold disgusted gaze travelling up and down my soiled wrinkled blue jeans and dusty boots and lighting with a kind of morbid satisfaction on my peeled and blistered nose.

"*We* thought you was somewhere in Europe, ma'am," Sergeant Buck said, grimly, out of one corner of his mouth. His lantern jaw jutted out menacingly.

"You mean you *wish* I were, Sergeant," I said. I wanted to add, "—and in a not very bomb-proof shelter," but I didn't quite dare, so I said, "No, we're here." I turned to my son. "You remember Sergeant Buck, don't you, dear?"

They shook hands just as Mrs. Chapman's voice came from across the lobby. "Come along, Grace. Our rooms are ready."

"We'll be seeing you," Bill said.

Sergeant Buck didn't answer. If he'd been outside I know he'd have spat neatly to the rear. Being inside, he just grunted and settled down to his paper again. And then something happened that I could never have believed. I glanced around at him as we followed the bellboy past the desk—and I got practically the greatest shock of my life. A large blonde —and I mean very blonde—woman in her middle thirties, I'd say, and in a pair of bright pink slacks, had got up from a desk by the window and was settling herself, comfortably and easily, in a chair beside him. And the shocking thing about it was that Sergeant Buck looked *pleased*. It was the first time in my long and always definitely grim association with him that I'd ever seen him look pleased about anything, or seen a woman with temerity enough to so much as speak to him, much less sit beside him.

"Oh my gosh, mother, get a load of that dame with old sour puss!" my son exclaimed, with the fine diction of the American upper classes.

"I already have," I said. "Hurry up, darling, and do wash your ears, and see if you can't comb your hair, just once."

5

The rooms Mrs. Chapman reserved for us were half-way down the long corridor past the elevator. Mine was on the Lake front next to Cecily's, and a room they'd converted into a sitting room separated hers from her grandmother's. George was across the hall from Mrs. Chapman, and Bill and Joe Anders, when he joined us, shared the one across from the sitting room, facing the enormous courtyard in back. The doors had transoms open to catch the cross breeze from the water, and the walls were no thicker than in most summer hotels. As I came into my room I could hear Cecily's whistling and running her tub on one side of me. On the other I heard a voice that had already become familiar.

"Quite a family party, eh, May?" Alexander Ridley remarked cheerfully. "Get me a fresh shirt, please, my dear.— No, a white one. Thank you. Take this one. Thank you, my dear."

"It's funny, meeting George here, isn't it," Mrs. Ridley said.

"With half a million people going through in a season, you're apt to meet most anybody," Mr. Ridley replied. "Cecily's certainly a beautiful girl. I wish Lisa had a little of her . . . 'charm' isn't quite the word . . . 'vitality' I suppose is better."

I turned on my bath and ostentatiously dropped my boots on the floor. They might as well know, I thought, that they were plainly audible. It didn't seem to impress them.

"I wonder if she's ever going to marry him," May Ridley said.

"I hope so. It would be an excellent connection. We could use a little of the Chapman and Davis business. If you can do a quiet build-up of your brother to old Mrs. Chapman, it might help things along. He'll never have a better chance than he's got right now."

There was a long silence. Then I heard Mr. Ridley say,

"Come away from that window and listen to me, my dear."

I rather wished at that point that I hadn't dropped my boots so loudly. This rift in the Ridley family was very interesting. For a moment I thought I'd heard the last of it, but Alexander Ridley went on.

"Now look, May—you're not using your head."

"I'm just thinking of——"

"You mean you're just not thinking," her husband interrupted curtly. "I'd be glad if you'd stop thinking about your brother and consider me for a minute . . . if that's not too much for a man to ask of his wife. We won't discuss the matter any more. George is going to marry Cecily if there's any way of making her have him. I expect you and Lisa to co-öperate—do you understand? I won't go into it. You know we've had a bad year. Chapman and Davis are going to have a brush with the S. E. C. and there's a good fat fee in it for somebody. George's connection with the firm isn't enough. If he makes a connection with the family, we're all set. George has a strong sense of clan. And it's time you were giving him a little encouragement, my dear. If there's any reason you don't like Cecily, I don't want to hear it.—I'm going out now and find out what's happened to Lisa. You can join me when you're ready."

I heard the hall door close; and after a moment, through the locked door that connected my room with theirs, I heard the sound of muffled sobs. Mrs. Ridley was crying. Then a door opened, and I heard a girl's voice exclaim,

"Mother—what is it, darling? What *is* the matter, mother?"

Mrs. Ridley spoke in a moment. "Nothing, Lisa. Nothing at all, dear. But listen—George is here, with that girl and her grandmother——"

"You mean *here?* At Lake? I thought he was at a ranch somewhere."

"They were—they're here now. And Lisa . . . please, darling, be as sweet to him as you can."

Lisa Ridley's voice was sharpened. "Look here, mother!"

"I know," her mother said hastily. "But you've got to be nice to them—for my sake."

"You mean for father's," Lisa Ridley retorted, her voice subdued and passionate. "I thought it was funny he decided to come here all of a sudden. All summer long, when I wanted to because Barbara and Dick were here in their trailer, we didn't have time, we had to hurry back to New York. I thought it was pretty strange he was so anxious for me to have fun with my cousins."

"Lisa, you aren't being fair!" her mother protested. "He didn't know they were going to be here. He really was thinking about your pleasure. And darling—you must promise me you'll be as nice as you can, to . . . everybody. It'll make it so much pleasanter."

I could feel the strained silence of the girl I'd never seen, and only pictured because I'd seen her mother and heard her father's unpaternal comment.

"All right," she said at last. "I've never seen Cecily Chapman and I haven't got anything against her. I just don't like the way Uncle George walks over everybody. I don't like the way he treats you. When Dick wanted to borrow five hundred dollars to finish his junior year, George was flat broke—but he stayed on the Riviera all summer, and he bought one of his rich friends a silver service for a wedding present. And do you know what he gave Barbara and Dick? He gave them a set of fish knives he got at the Flea Fair in Paris, and fish gives Barbara hives. I don't like my Uncle George . . . but I'll be nice to him if it kills me, if it's going to save you anything. So buck up, darling, and let me do something to your hair. And after dinner let's go see Barbara and Dick. They're at the trailer camp near the Ranger Station. They're having all kinds of fun!"

The Ridley family were curiouser and curiouser, I thought, and my bath was stone cold.

My first glimpse of Lisa Ridley came about an hour later. I'd gone along to the lobby to meet Colonel Primrose, to take him to Mrs. Chapman's sitting room for a cocktail before dinner. It was very nice seeing him again, and there was something warm and reassuring about having him there. He looked extremely fit. His bland genial face was as brown as leather. The peace-time twinkle in his black eyes was so disarming that I forgot for the moment how sharp and X-raying they were underneath, and how little they missed, and how seldom they revealed what they saw.

"What I want to know," I demanded before we'd even finished shaking hands, "is *who* is Sergeant Buck's lady friend?"

He laughed.

"Her name is Pearl—Pearl St. John," he answered, a little wryly. "Don't ask me where she got it. All I can tell you about her is that the poor little woman has had two husbands who were brutes and robbed her unmercifully, and as Buck himself has remarked in another connection, there's no fool like an old fool."

He smiled, and since his self-styled "functotum" had made that remark in reference to his colonel's supposed infatuation with me, the implication was clear enough.

"However," he said, "it's you I'm interested in. How was the trip?"

"Marvellous," I replied. "It couldn't have been nicer."

Perhaps my bath, or the distance that separated us from the solitary ghost in the Thorofare, explained my renewed enthusiasm. At any rate I only had that momentary twinge that comes with any overstatement.

"You're coming along now to meet the Chapmans . . . and George."

"George?"

He took the name up sharply, as if he'd misunderstood my special emphasis and thought it was personal.

"George Pelham," I said. "He's the canker in the heart of the rose. Our side doesn't want Cecily Chapman to marry him. His side's been numerically weak, but he's got reinforcements. A busload of his relatives arrived the same time we did. But come along. You'll see."

It seems to me now that I'd have done a neater job of things if I'd gone and got a glass bulb of assorted pestilences and taken it in with me instead. But Colonel Primrose *looked* so like somebody you could safely introduce to your friends that I forgot, for the moment, that my earliest encounter with him had been in a casual civilized group of people having a cocktail before dinner, and had ended in an apalling mess with nobody knowing who he was planning to hang next.

We opened the door of Mrs. Chapman's sitting room and went in. I introduced him. I was glad, somehow, he hadn't seen Mrs. Chapman first in her faded blue specially-cut ranch regalia and battered ten gallon hat. Not that she was any less formidable in the bright purple and white print dress she wore now, but she didn't look quite so much as if her six-shooter was smoking. And they took to each other just as instantly, it seemed to me, as he and Alexander Ridley didn't. George he seemed unusually casual about, and Cecily only proved what Sergeant Buck had warned me against very early in my association with them: "Don't trust him, ma'am —he's always been a fool for a pretty face."

He was talking to Mrs. Chapman when Lisa Ridley came in. I put down my glass and looked at her with more curiosity than was polite. She wasn't "vital," I suppose, but she had curly hair that stood out around her delicate pointed features like a soft cloud of dark smoke. Her eyes were mossy grey, and the rest of her face quite colorless except for the dark orange lipstick she wore. She was slight and rather frail, and could have had a rare kind of elfin piquancy, I thought, if she hadn't been dressed in a mousy brown jersey suit halfway to her ankles with a mustard blouse that made her skin sallow and lifeless.

She stood uncertainly in the doorway, the only live thing about her her quite extraordinary eyes. They seemed more frightened than anything else.

Mrs. Chapman put down the ice tongs.

"Is this Lisa?"

Her voice was not as brusque and grim as it ordinarily was.

A quick answering little smile lighted the girl's face. She took a shy step forward, and stopped abruptly, the smile wiped out in a flash, as her father moved out and intercepted her.

"Go wash your face before you appear in public, my dear," he said, in a bantering humorous voice, propelling her playfully back through the door. "Your mother doesn't approve of lipstick on children."

An audible gasp came from somewhere in the room—from me, probably. At any rate I caught one glimpse of that child's face as she flashed the back of her hand to her mouth and turned and fled, scarlet-faced, down the hall. I could cheerfully have boiled Mr. Alexander Ridley in oil. He turned to his wife, who was already practically effaced in a chair in the corner.

"My dear, you'll have to keep a sharper eye on your daughter."

"You're a fool, Mr. Ridley," Mrs. Chapman said curtly. "Why shouldn't the child use lipstick? Look at my granddaughter. Looks like a traffic light."

Mr. Ridley couldn't have been blander. "But that's quite different, Mrs. Chapman. It's becoming to her. Lisa's not the type."

"Rot," said Mrs. Chapman. Her frosty old eyes were snapping like sparks from a steel crucible.

"Lisa is pretty young for that sort of thing," George said casually, shaking the olive out of his glass into his mouth.

Cecily got up. Her cheeks were flushed and her eyes smoldering. "I'm going out a while, grandmother," she said. "Excuse me, will you?"

Mrs. Ridley sat there quietly, her cocktail untouched on the table beside her. I saw her husband take it and leave his own empty glass in its place. She looked at it, and then looked down at her hands folded in her lap.

Lisa didn't come back. I saw her when she came in to dinner behind her father and mother, her eyes down, a curious flushed pallor in her face.

"They make me sick," Cecily remarked. "Can't you do something about it, George? They don't let her move by herself."

"She's just a kid," George said.

"She's nineteen," Mrs. Chapman said. "I was married and had a baby when I was nineteen."

After dinner, when they were moving the chairs into place for a lecture on the geysers of Yellowstone, we were sitting over in front of the great log fire. Bill had picked up another boy and they'd gone out for a speedboat ride in the moonlight. George was over at the desk sending off telegrams. Cecily and Lisa came in with their coats on.

"Lisa and I are going over to the trailer camp to see her cousins," Cecily announced, kissing her grandmother lightly on the cheek.

"Now, now, Cecily," Mr. Ridley said pleasantly. "Lisa wants to hear the lecture."

"No, I don't!" Lisa Ridley blurted out breathlessly.

"Oh yes you do, my dear. Your mother doesn't allow you out at night unchaperoned. And anyway, Cecily and George want a little time alone together."

Mrs. Chapman gave me a sardonic smile.

"Mrs. Latham will go along and chaperone the girls, Mr. Ridley," she said dryly—and rather more briskly than usual. "The colonel can go too to make it doubly safe. George can make a fourth at bridge. I'm too old to listen to lectures on anything, and so are you. Now run along, all of you, and have fun. Take the car, Cecily. And remember the roads are patrolled by handsome rangers."

I glanced back at her as we went, sitting composedly between Lisa's parents—Mrs. Ridley grateful but anxious, her husband neatly checkmated but taking it with excellent grace. There was nothing about the grim square-jawed old lady that looked particularly like the instrument of fate just then. I still wonder sometimes whether if she'd known what she was sending us out to she wouldn't have done it just as calmly. I don't know, and it's too late to ask her now.

There was certainly nothing ominous in the dazzling moonlit lake lying shimmering through the dark pines as we went across the narrow wooden bridge from the rear courtyard into the Loop road. We could hear the subdued roar of the speedboat and see the white flashing spray as it zoomed across the glassy glittering surface of the water. We heard the tedious put-a-put-a-put of the white government launch die as it nosed into the dock along the shore. An open green patrol car passed us, the ranger at the wheel grinning cheerfully at the two bareheaded girls in the front seat of Mrs. Chapman's ancient vehicle that might have been called a jalopy if it hadn't cost at least ten thousand when it was new and wasn't still a lovely shiny red.

"They have to pass a screen test to get a job here, you know," Cecily said. Lisa giggled. Away from her father she was as different as a water lily closed at night and opened to the sun in the daylight.

"You'll love Barbara and Dick, Cecily," she said. "Dick's family lives in Mexico. They gave them a trailer for a wedding present and they're going home by way of Alaska. They're having such fun! I sneaked off to see them this afternoon. I was scared I wasn't going to get to see them at all. Our bus leaves at nine in the morning and I knew it would take a miracle to get me out tonight. Your grandmother's wonderful!"

"She's a lamb in a tiger skin," Cecily said warmly. "I adore her."

We were moving slowly along the hard surfaced road by the lake shore. Little groups of savages—which is what they call the college students the lodges employ for the summer— strolled along the shoulders, in twos if they were mixed, or in fours and fives until they came together and paired like paramœcia under a microscope. We passed the store with the grotesque fretwork of knotted pine branches over the porch —and why anyone should think a tree in the throes of arthritis is decorative I wouldn't know. Back in the tall sparse woods we could see the fires in the trailer camp. Ahead of us was the low log cabin with the bleached elk antlers over the door, that seemed from the two I'd already seen to mark a Ranger Station or a snowshoe cabin. The door was open. Half a dozen boys in the blue denim work uniform of the

CCC were clustered around it. They grinned and waved at the two girls, saw the colonel and me and subsided instantly.

"Let's go on up to Fishing Bridge and back," Cecily said, speeding up, and slowing down abruptly when two red lamps in the middle of the road materialized into an elk and practically sent us into the ditch. "No, I think we won't," she said. "Let's go back. I want to get a map at the Ranger Station."

She laughed. "Maybe we can pick up a glamorous ranger for you, Lisa."

"Father would die!" Lisa exclaimed.

"He won't know about it," Cecily said calmly. "Maybe I'll know somebody there. I do have to get a map for grandmother."

She turned, and we were going back again, just as the green patrol car came back with two rangers in it, their hats plainly identifying them in the light from the door as they got out and began to unload a duffel bag from the back seat. Cecily pulled up between the lodgepole pines and stopped.

"I don't suppose you girls would like me to get it for you?" Colonel Primrose remarked. They both laughed and scrambled out.

"Ranger," Colonel Primrose called. "May these young ladies have a map?"

The nearest of the two pulling stuff out of the patrol car turned and saw Cecily, and Lisa just behind her. His face lighted up amazingly.

"You bet," he said. "Come on in."

The other ranger straightened up, and turned around. And he stood there, as if turned to solid rock, his eyes fixed over the shoulder of his mate on the slim bright-haired girl facing him in the headlights of the two cars.

Cecily didn't move. Her feet, one advanced in front of the other, froze in a step half-taken. One hand raised a little was poised motionless like a hand cut from marble.

The other ranger, the smile gone suddenly from his face, stared at her, and then back at Steven Grant behind him. He took off his hat and said, "Sam, what the hell's the—," and then stopped and moved out of the way, his face a troubled earnest blank.

I leaned back against the cold leather cushion of the car and closed my eyes. Colonel Primrose had bent forward, his eyes intent. Lisa was just standing there, her lips parted, her eyes wide open, one hand still clinging to Cecily's. I opened my eyes again. Lisa's hand had fallen from Cecily's, and Cecily was moving forward . . . so slowly that I hardly realized at first she was moving at all, until she was only a step away from him.

She raised her hand slowly to touch him, still not believing—fearing, it seemed to me, that the figure standing there so motionless would vanish, intangible and uncorporeal, materialized out of her own deep longing.

"Steve," she whispered. Her trembling fingers touched his arm. *"Steve!"*

Her voice rose as if touching him had shocked the cry out of the deepest recesses of her heart.

"Cecily!"

Her name broke through the numb aching lips that must have whispered it a thousand times, the last twenty-four hours. He took a step forward.

"Listen, Cecily!"

Then in an instant so lightning that it seemed to annihilate time and space, Cecily flashed backward. She was like a living flame, every fibre of her burning with white hot unquenchable fire. For an instant I waited for the fiery torrent of words I knew must come to burst out, molten, volcanic. But I was wrong. She stood an instant, her chin up, her eyes like dark flaming stars, her foot on the running board, waiting for Lisa, frightened and shaken, to crawl in. Then she slipped lightly under the wheel and turned on the ignition. She turned her head.

"Goodbye, Steve," she said, her voice like water dropping from an icicle. "Good luck!"

Her racing motor roared through the stunned silence, drowning out anything Steve Grant might have said. But I don't think there was anything to drown. I don't think he could have spoken if his life depended on it—and it did, I thought, watching him standing there on the spot where Cecily had flamed up like the Phœnix from the trembling ashes of unbelief and doubt. His powerful hands were still stretched out, his face terrible with the dumb agony of the damned. I didn't dare turn and look at him as the big car gathered speed along the road. It had all happened, and was over, with such shattering swiftness, out of nothing at all . . . and happened so much worse than I could have believed it might, leaving no chance to escape it ever.

6

I was so torn to bits I was hardly aware of the breakneck speed we were going at, until I heard Colonel Primrose's voice saying quietly, "Not so fast, Miss Cecily," and her clipped controlled answer.

"I'm sorry." She slowed down. "—Now, darling, where's the trailer?"

Lisa's stricken little voice was hardly audible.

"You . . . don't want to bother, Cecily. Let's just . . . just go back."

Anybody who says Spartan breeding—as of ladies gay at supper, their crinolines concealing death eating the last torn remnants of their hearts—died with the old South is crazy. Except for that one burst of speed there was nothing to reveal the blinding agony that was tearing Cecily Chapman in shreds.

"Don't be silly," she said. Only my ears, attuned for days to the rippling velvety undertones of her voice, could know how torn they were now. "That was . . . just a man I hadn't expected to see . . . out here."

She didn't know, of course, that I knew. That came to me as a shock—I'd been so intimately involved with it now for days, it seemed to me.

We were going slowly through the winding road of the trailer camp. The smoke from the pinewood fires rose eerily into the silver-tipped tree tops.

"There they are!" Lisa cried.

A gleaming new trailer with Chinese red venetian blinds was drawn up in a tiny grove. A man and girl were sitting in gay red and white canvas chairs beside a camp table under a red and white awning stretching from the side of the trailer. The girl was fluffy-haired and blonde, the man was tall and dark, with a candid open face and nice blue eyes. He was hunched comfortably down on the small of his back, the smoke curling contentedly up from his pipe.

"Hello, Lisa!"

They both jumped up and welcomed us like royal nomads to a desert tent. Their name was Winston, it seemed, and they were having a wonderful time. A bear had got their bacon the night before, and a can of syrup the night before that, and torn up Barbara's Parisian straw hat, thinking the flowers were edible, this very morning. It was great fun. Their chatter whirred through the palsied turmoil of my brain like the ball bearings of a dynamo, Cecily's faster and brighter than all the rest, until I thought I'd go mad listening to them.

Suddenly Cecily got to her feet. I don't know how long it had been. It seemed hours to me. She held out her hand to Barbara and Dick, and turned to me.

"Here are the keys, Grace. Will you drive back, after a while? I'm going to walk."

Lisa started to get up, understood and settled down again. Colonel Primrose got up too, but didn't offer to go along. I was glad, because I don't think she could have said another word without her whole brittle façade crumpling into a mass of ruins.

"Righto," I said. She started off. After a moment I heard her quick steps break into a run.

Dick Winston took his pipe out of his mouth. "Anything wrong?" he asked.

"No," Lisa said primly. "It's just that her grandmother's an awful tartar and she doesn't like to be out late."

I didn't know whether I wanted to laugh or cry. It seemed such a gallant absurd defense, and pathetic because it jumped so instantly to her mind out of her own experiences in the war between parents and children.

We stayed on in front of the Winstons' camp fire fifteen minutes or so longer, I should imagine. It seemed more like fifteen hours to me, with the sound of Cecily's blind running feet still beating in my ears, underlining the magpie chatter of Lisa and her cousins. A mutual objection to their Uncle George seemed to sew them together in stitches of merriment. And every time I happened to glance at Colonel Primrose he was regarding me with thoughtful eyes through the fragrant cloud of smoke from the wedding cigar Dick had dispensed.

Lisa, with the sublime capacity of the very young, had forgotten the entire incident—or so I'd thought, not realizing how thoroughly she'd been trained to cloak and dissemble in the face of society. Her small hushed voice asking, "Was . . . I mean, do you suppose that could have been Steve *Grant* she . . . we saw?" as I manœuvred the big red car out of the trailer camp came to me as a distinct shock. All the while she'd been chattering away by the Winstons' fire she must have been busily searching a past that she could hardly have been old enough to know much about. The blatant raucous voice of an electric phonograph from the store blared out "Seafood, Mamma!" into the silent moon-drenched night. I nodded my head.

"But I . . . I thought he was supposed to have been . . . killed," she said. "And that's how George——"

I glanced quickly in the windshield mirror and gave her a sharp kick with the toe of my shoe to shut her up. Whatever the infirmities of my friend Colonel Primrose, relaxed comfortably with his cigar in the back seat—and they include a stiff neck from a bullet in the Argonne and a rheumatic knee that sometimes creaks when he kneels down to inspect a corpse or a clue—deafness is not one of them. There was no sign in his face that he had heard, much less understood—which, as I knew very well, was no sign he'd not done both.

Lisa started a little guiltily and bit her lip.

"It gets very cold up here when the sun goes down, doesn't it, Mrs. Latham," she said, brightly.

"Yes, it does," I said.

I could have wrung her precious little neck. Even if the motor hadn't coughed and almost died while I was trying to get my foot through the maze of unfamiliar brakes and gears back on the accelerator, that would have been much more than enough to convince Colonel Primrose we were trying to conceal something from him.

"I expect it's the altitude," Lisa said. "They say the lake used to be a hundred and sixty feet higher than it is now, in the last glacial epoch—or something, and it flowed out the other way, and that's why they have cutthroat trout in the upper Missouri waters and not any place else east of the Divide. At least that's what the man said at Old Faithful last night. It's a lovely night, isn't it?"

"Yes, it is," I said. I glanced again at Colonel Primrose in the mirror. He had such a perfectly maddening twinkle in his shrewd black eyes that perturbed as I was it took me a definite effort to keep from laughing.

I pulled the long car up behind the hotel and switched the lights off quickly to spare the sensibilities of a woman undressing in the dark without drawing the shade in a window three feet from the ground in front of our headlights. Colonel Primrose got out and opened the door for Lisa. She gave us a breathless "Thank you—I've had a lovely time!" and dashed into the hotel. Colonel Primrose waited for me to get out and closed the door.

"Now, what's this all about, Mrs. Latham?" he inquired, patiently.

"Nothing," I said.

He looked quietly at me for an instant.

"You mean, a certain Steve gets killed, and comes to life as Sam, just in the ordinary course of human events?"

"I mean it's nothing that's anybody's business except Steve's—and Cecily's," I said. "*Believe* me, it isn't. And anyway, you're on a vacation. Had you forgotten?"

"I thought something was bothering you, this afternoon," he said irrelevantly. He held the screen door open for me to go inside.

The lecture was over. The orchestra was playing sedately and a few people were dancing where the Filipino boys had pulled the chairs away and rolled up the rugs. I looked over to see if my son was among them, and gave a startled audible gasp. The large perspiring granite monolith figure of Sergeant Buck was gliding—or something—by in the smiling tow of the lady known as Pearl. She was guiding him as expertly as a tug docking the old *Majestic* in the cramped quarters of the North River, and she supported him as he caught sight of me and the Colonel, turned as brassy red as an overheated cauldron, stumbled and went doggedly on behind the merciful seclusion of a large square pillar.

"Well," I said.

Colonel Primrose gave me an only half-amused smile. "I . . . think I'll have a scotch and soda," he said. "Will you join me?"

"No, thanks," I said. "I'm going to bed. I'll see you in the morning."

Actually I never felt less like bed in my life. But I wanted desperately to get rid of him. I had to see Mrs. Chapman before Cecily got back, to prepare her for whatever shock must come.

Colonel Primrose gave me a formal little bow. "Good night, Mrs. Latham," he said. "Don't be impulsive, will you."

He looked at me again, and smiled faintly. "Good night."

I retreated hastily around the corner of the transportation desk and started along the hall. I wasn't being impulsive, I thought—and if I'd allowed myself to be the night before, and told Mrs. Chapman what I knew, as I should have done, a lot of this might somehow have been avoided. As I passed the telegraph bureau, the girl in charge looked up and said, "Wait a minute, will you?"

I stopped and came back. She fished a couple of blanks out of the wire basket on her table and brought them over to the counter.

"You're with Mrs. Chapman's party, aren't you?"

I nodded.

"The gentleman with you turned these in. He forgot to sign them, and I don't know his name. I wonder if you'd give it to me so I can send them off before I close up."

I glanced down at the two forms—and my eyes stayed glued to the neatly printed words on the yellow paper. My heart gave a sudden jolt to the pit of my stomach, my knees were so unsteady I had to lean against the desk.

> STATES ATTORNEY
> MECKLENBURG COUNTY
> MECKLENBURG DELAWARE
> HAVE REASON TO BELIEVE BODY OF MAN BURNED CAR
> CHAPMANS LANE MAY 16 1936 NOT STEVEN GRANT BUT
> JOHN C BRICE FORMERLY EMPLOYED CHAPMAN AND DAVIS
> 30 BROAD STREET N Y C RESIDING AT THAT DATE DAVEN-
> PORT HOTEL 46TH STREET N Y C STOP SUGGEST INVESTIGA-
> TION BE OPENED

The other one was shorter.

> SECRETARY OF INTERIOR
> WASHINGTON D C
> LOCAL RUMOR RANGER SAM GRAHAM YELLOWSTONE PARK
> SERVICE GOING BY ASSUMED NAME STOP SUGGEST IMME-
> DIATE INQUIRY

Neither of them was signed. The picture of George chewing his pencil at the desk while Mrs. Chapman and Cecily were bludgeoning Mr. Ridley into allowing Lisa to visit her cousins in the trailer camp flashed into my mind. He must have finished them at just about the time Cecily stood face to face with the man they were designed to hurt.

I heard the girl in front of me through a blur of dismay and anger that amounted almost to despair.

"I tried to locate him, but I couldn't," she was saying anxiously. "He signed the first drafts he made. And I shouldn't think anybody would want to send that kind of messages without signing them, would you?"

"No," I said, as calmly as I could. "Not Mr. Pelham, anyway. Let me have them."

I picked up a pencil and scrawled "George Pelham" at the bottom of each of them, and put his room number at the side. If I was breaking any established law other than one of etiquette, I didn't know it and I didn't care. George was betraying an old friend. I couldn't prevent that, but I could stop him from doing it anonymously and getting off scot-free from the consequences.

The girl took them and smiled uncertainly. "Thank you," she said. "I didn't like to send them without some kind of signature."

"I'm sure Mr. Pelham just forgot," I said. "You know how men are."

"I should say I do," she laughed. "You see all kinds in a job like this. But I guess it takes all kinds to make a world."

"I guess it does," I agreed. I didn't add that there were some kinds the world could get along without very nicely, and that as far as I was concerned George Pelham was one of them.

"Good night," she said. I said "Good night" and hurried along past the open door of the shoe shining booth where the long row of our dusty boots stood, sort of wearily empty. I could hear the click-click-clickety-click of the telegraph transmitter back of me, methodically ticking out impending doom. My cheeks were burning like fire, my hands were as cold as ice.

I hurried along the hall beside the long narrow library lounge. It seemed incongruous and absurd that so many people could be so placidly engaged in sending post cards of bears and geysers back to Iowa and Alabama and Oregon . . . having a lovely time . . . wish you were here. I wished all of them were here just then instead of me—and George Pelham. I would have liked to be at home in Georgetown, and as for George, I wished he were in the seventh circle of Dante's Inferno.

Ahead of me beyond the big green sofa at the end of the main wing I heard the door in the transverse hall in front of the elevator open and slam shut. I stopped short as I recognized the girl who came suddenly into view and broke into a run up the short flight of carpeted steps that led to the extended level our rooms were on. I tried to call, but she didn't hear me. I quickened my pace. If I could only catch up with her before she reached her grandmother's sitting room! But I knew I couldn't, she was going too rapidly. She reached the door and stopped just as I hurried up the stairs. She didn't look around; she just stood an instant, her hand on the knob, her head thrown back a little, her chin up.

"Cecily!" I called.

She didn't hear me. The next instant she was gone, and I

heard the door close quietly behind her. I ran the rest of the way, sick with dread. At the door I stopped. I could hear her voice through the open transom, calm and cool and under complete control.

"Grandmother," she said. "I want you to know I've decided to marry George . . ."

I leaned against the door frame, really more sea-sick than I've been on the ocean, my throat aching horribly. Some people coming out of another room looked at me oddly. I knew I couldn't stand there any longer, so I opened the door as quietly as I could and slipped inside.

Cecily was standing in the middle of the floor, her face as white as parchment, her head erect, her dark amber-flecked eyes clear and very bright. Her grandmother, a card in her hand frozen motionless half-way to the board, her lips as blue as sudden indigo, was staring at her, speechless. George Pelham, across the table from his sister, his face a complex mask of surprise and bewilderment, had risen half to his feet, obviously not believing his ears.

Cecily's voice, with not a break to indicate she'd heard the door open or that she was in any way aware of anybody's presence behind her, went on steadily.

"—Right away. The end of the week—as soon as I've talked to father on the telephone."

George's face lighted. He sprang around behind his sister's chair and caught her in his arms. Mrs. Chapman's hand dropped to the table. She closed her eyes, her lips pressed together in a tragic bitter line.

"Cecily, my dear—tell me again you mean it!"

George's lips were muffled against her hair. Cecily stood rigidly erect, her head forward against his shoulder, nodding slowly. And then George did a surprising thing. He released her almost abruptly and started for the door.

"I'll be back in a minute. I sent a telegram to the office. It hasn't any point now and perhaps it hasn't gone. I'll see if I can stop it."

He was gone. I sat down weakly in the nearest chair. Alexander Ridley smiled at his wife across the corner of the table.

7

"Grandmother!" Cecily's voice vibrated with alarm and entreaty. She took a quick step toward the old lady, sagging blue-lipped and defeated against the back of her chair, and checked herself sharply as the square old jaw snapped back into place. Mrs. Chapman stiffened, her body erect in the chair, a grim hard-bitten old dowager again, every muscle under iron control. She flicked the ace of spades still in her hand down onto the unfinished play in the middle of the board.

"Our trick, Mr. Ridley," she said curtly. "Game and rubber."

She picked up her pencil and finished off the score.

Cecily drew back, her lips quivering, like a thoroughbred lashed across the face by a trusted friend. She stood an instant, her breath coming in strangled hurt little gusts, then turned and fled through the door into her own room. It slammed shut behind her. Mrs. Chapman gathered up the cards, her fingers brisk, her lips a hard line drawn tightly down at the corners.

"You can pay your husband, Mrs. Ridley," she said. "George can settle with me."

Mr. Ridley smiled. "—I'm afraid that sounds a little ominous, if I may say so, Mrs. Chapman," he remarked facetiously.

I thought so too, and I wasn't trying to be funny.

Mrs. Chapman pushed her chair back.

"In any event," she said calmly, "my position is perfectly clear. I've always been opposed to my granddaughter's marrying your brother-in-law, Mr. Ridley. Nothing has happened this evening to make me change my mind."

I took a deep breath. So much had happened that she didn't know about. What effect any of it would have on her when she did know it—as she must any moment now—I didn't dare to think.

She got up, bracing herself a moment with her fingertips on the green felt-topped table. "Good night, Mrs. Ridley, and Mr. Ridley. Thank you both."

They got up, Mr. Ridley at ease and very much satisfied, Mrs. Ridley more shadowy and effaced than ever in the bright penumbra of his confident ego.

"Good night, Mrs. Chapman," he said. His tone was quite kindly. "We're all of us here old enough and wise enough—and experienced enough, I believe—to know the folly of trying to stand in the way of young love."

I closed my eyes to establish at least a personal blackout before the bombs began to crash. Mrs. Chapman's infinite patience was certainly as trigger-quick and combustible as that of any better known but further removed dictator. It won't be long now, I thought—but nothing came, not even the muted snort she sometimes gave instead of her sharp "Nonsense!" that my son's brief "Nuts!" would seem to put more succinctly.

The door closed without incident, I opened my eyes and got up.

"Stay where you are," Mrs. Chapman said peremptorily. She turned the key in the lock and glanced up at the open transom. "See if you can close that, first."

I closed it and sat down again. I hadn't felt so much like a child who'd broken her great-great-grandmother's Crown Derby soup tureen and tried vainly to fib her way out of it since I'd done just that at the age of six. And furthermore, my unfortunate complicity in the matter of the telegrams had definitely changed my whole moral position in this ghastly business.

Mrs. Chapman sat down, facing me grimly.

"What happened?—There's no use trying to soften it. You ought to know me well enough by now to know that."

I did try to soften it, however. The picture of her in a state of approaching collapse in her chair was too alarming for me to want to repeat it—not without some kind of preparation.

"It's much more staggering than you can conceive of, Mrs. Chapman," I said earnestly.

She looked at me with those shrewd blue icicle eyes. In the instant before they focussed steady and unflinching on mine I saw them run a swift gamut of fears.

"Go on," she said.

"It's Steve, Mrs. Chapman."

She stared at me silently for a moment. *"Steve?"*

I nodded.

"He isn't dead. He's alive—here in the Park. Cecily met him."

Her face was still blank and uncomprehending, her hands motionless on her lap.

"It's quite true, Mrs. Chapman," I said, as steadily as I could.

"I don't believe it," she said curtly.

"I'm sorry," I said. "It's *quite* true. He's a ranger—here in Yellowstone."

"You're perfectly mad," Mrs. Chapman said. "Steve was killed in a motor accident three years ago. Anyway, he was lame. He couldn't be a ranger. Cecily's lost her mind."

She got up and started briskly toward the door leading to her granddaughter's room.

"*Mrs. Chapman!*" I said. My voice must have had more authority than I'd have believed possible, because she stopped abruptly and turned. "—Sit down, please. You've got to listen and understand. Cecily hasn't lost her mind at all. Steve *is* alive. He was the ranger in the Thorofare. George recognized a picture of him when they went to register us at the ranger station Saturday. He met him in the snowshoe cabin on Cabin Creek. I heard them talking. He told him you and Cecily were down by the river—that's why Steve didn't come down, and why he left so abruptly, and why he didn't come over on the boat with us this afternoon. There's no possible doubt about it; Cecily spoke to him, he spoke to her. It's incredible, unbelievable—but it's a fact."

Mrs. Chapman moved back and sat down, hardly aware, I think that she was doing it. Her breath came slowly, in deep tortured waves, raising and lowering the big bunch of purple velvet pansies on her bosom.

"Get me my smelling salts out of that drawer," she said.

I went over to the wicker table in front of the windows and pulled the drawer open. Lying on top of a pile of hotel stationery was a small green bottle with white crystals in it. I picked it up. As I did I touched the cold numbing blue steel of George's revolver lying there beside it—still unsealed, looking even more menacing now than it had at the foot of the dark fringe of trees that separated our camp fire from the tiny snowshoe cabin in the lonely clearing in the wilderness.

I closed the drawer and went back across the room with the bottle of smelling salts. Mrs. Chapman held it to her nose, breathing it slowly, her eyes fixed in front of her, her jaws clamped, grim and unrelenting as a steel bear trap. She didn't speak for a long time. The room was so silent I could hear my watch ticking on my wrist, my heart beating inside of me. Then, after hours, it seemed to me, she said quietly, "I still don't believe it, Grace."

"In that case," I said, a little more tartly than I'd meant to, "you ought to do something about it. George wired the States Attorney in Delaware that the body in the burned car was probably John Brice's, and the Secretary of the Interior that the Thorofare ranger known as Sam Graham was in fact somebody else going under an assumed name."

She stared at me, her face suddenly concentrated and alive again, her eyes burning frosty blue fire. She put her bottle of smelling salts on the bridge table and got to her feet.

"—Listen, Grace. I told you once that Steve Grant was the finest human being I ever knew or hope to know. I said he couldn't do anything that was ungallant, ungenerous or dishonorable. I still say it."

Her voice vibrated with passionate affirmation. She stood there facing me, her eyes blazing with almost savage conviction.

"And now—where is he? Bring him here. I want to see him, at once!"

I picked up my coat and put it on. "I'll see if I can find him," I said dubiously. "If he hasn't disappeared again. Cecily didn't leave him much choice in the matter."

"Find him," Mrs. Chapman said peremptorily. "If you can't do it, get your friend the Colonel to help you. He's a professional at that sort of thing, isn't he?"

"Only a gifted amateur, unless the government's involved," I said, very keenly aware that if the government wasn't involved just then, it would be by the time George's telegram to the Secretary reached its destination. I unlocked the door and opened it. "He ought to be kept out of this as long as possible," I added, "—if anybody wants any peace around here."

"I don't want peace—I want the truth," Mrs. Chapman retorted imperiously. "Take the car and don't come back till you find him."

It seemed to me just off-hand, as I hurried down the hall, that it was one of those things much simpler to order done than to do. Even if I found Steve, who didn't know me from Adam, I had no assurance I could bring him back alive. I could very easily imagine him thinking Daniel's visit to the lions' den was a pleasant afternoon at the zoo compared with facing Mrs. Chapman at the Lake Hotel just then. Moreover, my geography in general tends to be definitely pre-Copernican, and concerning Yellowstone Park specifically it wasn't even as advanced as that. If Steve had left the Lake Ranger Station I might as well plan to spend the night, I figured, in the first comfortable tree I could find that a bear couldn't. I certainly wouldn't have courage to face Mrs. Chapman empty-handed.

I hurried down the short steps to the lobby level and slowed down hastily. At the far end of the library lounge Mr. Ridley was seated on the long highbacked green sofa, talking earnestly to George Pelham. My heart sank to my heels so that they beat a louder clatter than ever on the polished floor covering as I tried to slip by without their seeing me. George must know by this time what I'd done, I reflected, and be ready to shoot me on sight.

He looked up as I passed. I smiled brightly. I might as well brazen it out, I thought, there being so little else I could do under the circumstances. To my mild dismay he smiled back quite as affably.

I glanced quickly at the telegraph office. George either was being as brazen as I was, which seemed incredible, or didn't yet know what I'd done. Then I remembered the girl had said she'd get his messages off before she closed up. And the office was closed. The pads and papers on the desk were neatly cleared away for the night, her chair was empty. In that case George and I could continue on friendly if not cordial terms till morning anyway, and what would happen after that I preferred not to look forward to. I was looking forward to plenty as it was—including, I suspected, a little difficulty in getting through the main lounge without being intercepted by Colonel Primrose.

But that situation was well under control. The Colonel's slightly rotund figure was securely and neatly cornered between a pillar and a tub of pink oleanders, a stag at bay . . . and the huntsman was none other than his own guard, philosopher and friend's Rubenesque lady friend Pearl. Whether or not she was still telling him the saga of her husbands I didn't know, but Colonel Primrose was plainly outflanked and outmanœuvred generally, and furthermore looked more acutely uncomfortable than it had ever been my pleasure to see him. I nodded sweetly to him. I could see from the sharpened inquiry in his eyes that while he hadn't been deceived by my fiction of going to bed, he hadn't expected me to be setting out alone again in the middle of the night. I saw him back away from Pearl, and I bolted out the door, half a dozen disturbed bats doing circles round my head, the howl of a lonely coyote coming from far away out of the night.

I got in the car and started it. As I backed out and shot forward down the road across the narrow wooden bridge toward the Loop road, I saw his solid figure outlined on the stoop. I realized I had to find a better way of avoiding him if and when I brought Steve Grant back, though I knew very well from experience that he already knew, as clearly as I did myself, precisely what I was up to. There's always something a little disconcerting about the role of open book, even though I'd played it often enough, heaven knew, in my dealings with him. With his private Ogpu in the toils of romance I'd thought I might reasonably expect to escape being circumvented at every crossroad the way I usually was.

The big red car—about as fitted for secret missions as a fire truck—gathered speed as I turned into the Loop road between the brilliantly lighted triple-pedimented hotel up the slope on my left and the lake gleaming vast and silvery on my right. I passed the Ranger Station. The door under the bleached branches of the elk antlers was closed, the only light I could see came from an inner room somewhere. I stood there undecided. I didn't somehow quite like to beat on the door shouting "Bring out your dead!" The silence that brooded over the whole place, intensified by the extraordinary incongruity of the electric phonograph blaring out down the road, would give any kind of summons a desperate urgency that I wanted to avoid. Anyway, Steve Grant wasn't dead. And if anybody constituted a plague it was George Pelham, comfortably back there in the library lounge . . . and at the moment he wasn't so much a plague as a gauntlet I'd have to run—again, if and when I found Steve Grant.

I went around the side of the low cabin. It was dark except where patches of moonlight through the pine tops wove a moving arabesque of black and silver on the dry sun-baked grass. There was no light in the windows just out of reach above my head. I went on around, and stopped uncertainly. I could hear a baby crying, a woman's voice speaking gently, a man saying "This little pig went to market." That couldn't be Steve Grant, I thought, or at least I hoped it couldn't. Anyway, I dashed back to the front of the place again and started around the other way. A light had come on in the windows at the end. I went up to the door there. It was marked "Private." It seemed to me I could hear the low murmur of a man's voice, so I knocked on the door. I waited a long time and knocked again, louder. I heard a chair move back and the heavy tread of boots, and the door opened. A huge ranger in uniform stood there, not beaming with cordiality but very polite.

"I'm awfully sorry to disturb you," I said. It was hard to

know exactly what to say. I had the awful feeling that I was going to be told Old Faithful wouldn't erupt again till morning and have the door closed on me, so I hurried breathlessly along, "Is Mr. Grant—I mean Mr. Graham—here? I have a message for him . . ."

The Ranger gave me a stare. "Who's calling, please?"

"Mrs. Latham—but the message is from Mrs. Chapman."

I heard some one else in the room get up abruptly. The Ranger at the door glanced back over his shoulder and turned to me again.

"Come in," he said.

He stepped aside and held the door open for me to enter . . . and I stood face to face with Steven Grant. That, of course, didn't surprise me. What did was that sitting on the maple Shaker sofa against the wall, and not calmly—anything but—was the small mouse-colored figure of Lisa Ridley, scared half out of her wits, her extraordinary eyes as big as saucers under her cloud of dusty hair.

8

Beside Lisa, with one of those young troubled faces that could never keep troubled more than five minutes at a time, no matter how hard its owner tried, was the other ranger who'd been present at the scene between Cecily and Steve. I stopped short, staring open-mouthed, I suppose, as I saw them, and Lisa got up quickly.

"Mrs. Latham, this is Monty." She indicated the young man beside her, and he grinned infectiously and held out his hand. "And this is Dutch," Lisa said, turning to the big blond giant who'd let me in. Then, as if a little shocked at her appalling familiarity—as I certainly was—she added primly, "He's the District Ranger."

How she'd got on such startlingly intimate terms with all of them in less than an hour was beyond me, but they didn't seem to be surprised, so I put it down to the great open spaces and let it go at that. She hesitated then. "—I don't know if you've met Steve," she said diffidently.

"No, I haven't," I said.

I turned back again and held out my hand. It was the first time I'd seen Steve Grant's face clearly. And when I looked at him, and in spite of anything, the sharp hot tears stung my eyelids. I saw so well just what Mrs. Chapman meant, and why. Nobody could have looked at those steady straightforward gray eyes, etched at the corners with suffering—and with laughter too, though certainly there was no laughter in them now—and thought of him as dishonorable, or looked at his mouth, big and flexible, set now in a tight grim line, and thought him ungenerous . . . or at his lean hard determined jaw and thought him a coward. His grip was warm and as firm as steel. There was no sign that I could see that his illness had left any mark on him, except in the lines at his eyes and the corners of his mouth, and in a kind of maturity and reserve force in his face that not many faces of young men have . . . and not many old ones.

"Mrs. Chapman wants to see you, Mr. Grant," I said.

A quick light, half pleasure, half distress, warmed his face for an instant, and died. He shook his head slowly. I didn't have the feeling that it was because he had any fear of seeing her at all. It was just that he'd gone over it thoroughly in his own mind already and rejected it—for what reasons I had no way of knowing.

The District Ranger pushed his chair across the Navajo rug to me and said, "I suggest we sit down and talk it over before you make up your mind . . ."

He hesitated as if he'd started to say "Sam," and stopped with it on the tip of his tongue.

I sat down. I was both startled and relieved. How much Dutch and Monty knew of what it was all about, I didn't know, but that they'd been discussing some aspects of it already was evident not only from that, but from Lisa's presence there and the silence that I'd walked in on.

Steve Grant stood for a moment, then sat down in his chair again. He hadn't spoken since I came in. It seemed to me for an instant that his jaw was so clamped that a word couldn't have got out of it if he'd wanted it to, but now he did speak, his words bitten off as if each one was harder and bitterer to get out than the one before it.

"There's nothing to talk over, Dutch. There's nothing I can . . . explain, not so anybody could understand. They'll just have to go on thinking I'm a first-rate—" He hesitated, out of politeness, I suppose. "—a first-rate so-and-so, and let it go at that."

He sat there, elbows propped on his knees, running his fingers through his short crisp hair, the muscles of his strong weather-beaten jaw and neck standing out in tense rigid lines. He raised his head and looked at me. If I ever saw living hell in anybody's eyes, it was in Steven Grant's then.

"Tell Mrs. Chapman I haven't anything to say," he said. He got up abruptly. "Only . . . tell her . . . Oh, hell, there's no use. I don't want to sound as if I'm trying to excuse myself."

"I think I'd see her if I were you, fella," Dutch drawled quietly. He knocked his pipe out against the polished calf of his boot and caught the dottle in the palm of his big hand. "Just because a man's a fool once isn't any sign he's got to go on being one, the way I look at it."

We sat there in a grim tense silence. Steve Grant moved from one side of the room to another like a caged tiger, lithe and lean and sinewy, with so faint a suggestion that he'd once been an ill man that I shouldn't have been aware of it if I hadn't known and was watching for it.

"There's no use," he said all of a sudden. "I talked to George. I tell you there's no use."

Lisa raised her head sharply.

"The more I hear about George," she said hotly, her cheeks flushing, "the more I think his fine Italian hand ought to be chopped off at the wrist."

Dutch looked at her in mild surprise, his match halted midway to his pipe.

"—Everybody knows George wouldn't go across the street to help his own mother if he was late for lunch."

"He's been swell to me," Steve said shortly.

"That's what you think!" Lisa retorted—taking, I may say, the words out of my own mouth, except that I don't think I was putting them quite that way.

"Look," Steve said patiently. "You don't know what you're talking about. George is O.K."

Lisa shrugged her shoulders and settled back against the cushion, her face a tight little wad of outraged futility.

I knew exactly how she felt. I gathered it wasn't the first time George's name had come up, and that nothing she'd said—knowing as little specifically as she did—had made the slightest dent in Steve's armor of loyalty. It made my job a little harder. If I did succeed in getting him to Mrs. Chapman and he'd got it into his head that George had everybody down on him, she'd put the finishing touch on that so thoroughly that nobody could ever convince him to the contrary. I slipped my coat off my shoulders and settled down in my chair.

"I hope," I said patiently, "there's an extra bed around here. Mrs. Chapman ordered me to bring you back to see her, and told me not to come back without you. I shouldn't particularly mind meeting a grizzly in the road, but frankly I'm just not up to Mrs. Chapman."

Steve Grant grinned suddenly, his whole face when he did lighting up as if with a battery of thousand-watt lamps.

"She hasn't changed, I guess," he said.

"She's worse," Lisa Ridley said—as firmly as if she'd known Mrs. Chapman for years instead of hours. She took a deep breath and shook her head. "It's a shame . . . because you know she . . . she can't live very long."

I stared at her dumbfounded. If anybody had the constitution of an ox it was the square-jawed old dowager back there at the hotel.

Then I understood as Steve said quickly, "What do you mean? She's not——"

Lisa nodded, shamelessly. "She's not very robust any more," she said simply. "Cecily's terribly upset. Isn't she, Mrs. Latham?"

I think one ought to lie when necessary, of course with extreme caution, but I didn't have to lie to nod my head in agreement with that. Cecily, I should say, was very much upset indeed, if not about her grandmother's health.

Steve turned to me. "I'll go, then," he said abruptly.

I put on my coat and glanced at Lisa. She sat there looking calmly up at the ceiling. If she'd ever heard of infant damnation she was quite undisturbed by it.

"Shall we go?" I said.

Dutch and Monty followed Steve into an adjoining room. Dutch closed the door. I could hear his slow Montana drawl, but I gathered that what he was saying was hardly to be taken literally, because there was no sound of any jaws being smashed, and there must have been if even the first three or four words had meant what they normally do. I went quickly over to Lisa.

"Listen, darling." I lowered my voice. "You come along, or go ahead if you can get your friend Monty to take you, and get Colonel Primrose and your Uncle George out of the lobby onto the front verandah while I take Steve to Mrs. Chapman. I don't want him to meet either of them."

"Oh, dear!" she whispered. "How'll I do it?"

I looked at her. "Listen, my pet," I said. "Just use any of your old methods, or think up a new one. I wouldn't presume to offer any suggestions."

She giggled irrepressibly. Then her face clouded. "—If father's not there," she said. Her voice quivered a little. "If he saw me with . . . with anybody, he'd make it ghastly. For mother, I mean—I don't care about myself."

She glanced quickly at the door. The knob was turning. "But I'll manage somehow," she whispered breathlessly.

The first part of it was so easy that it may have been arranged already—I wouldn't pretend to know. Anyway, Monty picked up his hat with a jaunty display of nonchalance that even Bill could have bettered. "If it's Okay, Dutch, I'll just take Miss Ridley down in my car. I have to go down to the Fisheries anyway. Okay?"

Dutch's smile was as slow and sardonic as his drawl.

"You be back here in ten minutes," he said. But Monty and Lisa had already disappeared. He went over to the door. "You heard what I said!" he bellowed, and looked around at me with a grin. "That ought to get him home by midnight." He turned to Steve then, his face suddenly sobered, and I saw him put his hand awkwardly on his shoulder. "Take it easy, fella," he said.

I got into the car, Steve beside me, hunched down in the leather seat. He didn't say anything for a while after I'd started off. Then he said, "She still snorts the same old way."

I straightened up, and relaxed. It was the car he was talking about, I realized with a certain amount of relief, not Mrs. Chapman. I said, "Yes." There were so many other things I'd have liked to say but none that I could. He wasn't the sort of person you could say anything to that he didn't want said. I was afraid that anything I might put in about George or Cecily would be just wrong.

We passed the gas station and the store in silence, and came in view of the big yellow and white hotel.

"How long have you been a ranger?" I asked suddenly. I hadn't meant to. It just popped out.

"I'm only a temporary," he answered, apparently not minding the question at all. "I was appointed about a month ago when the Ranger down in Thorofare had to have his appendix taken out. I was a fire lookout before that, up at Pelican Cone. I was there all last summer."

"That must be a pretty lonely job," I said. Then I thought "Oh Lord, what a thing to say," and made it worse by adding, "I mean off by yourself on top of a mountain."

"It gives you a lot of time to think," he said quietly.

A rattle-trap car coming down the hotel drive came to a stop, the brakes screeching like a carload of brazen-throated parrots. Monty behind the wheel stood halfway up, grinning at us over the top of the cracked sticker-plastered windshield. We turned into the road to the parking yard in back of the hotel. Lisa wouldn't have had much time to do her job, I thought, wondering for a moment whether I ought to give her more. Then I figured it would be easier to get them out onto the porch than keep them there after she'd got them, so I put my foot on the gas and speeded up across the wooden bridge around the kitchen into the court. I parked against the log curb, and Steve and I got out.

We hurried across the dusty yard to the back door and into the lobby. I gave a long breath of relief. Not only were George and Colonel Primrose not in the lounge—nobody was, not even a bellboy. Everybody was crowded out on the porch. I heard a woman's voice saying sharply, "Where are they? I don't see any moose! She must be crazy!"

"Come along!" I said to Steve quickly. If the woman didn't see any, Colonel Primrose certainly wouldn't—and no one would be quicker to smell a rat. Our feet echoed alarmingly along the empty narrow corridor. I looked back as we reached the steps to the other level. People were crowding into the lobby. I saw the Colonel's substantial figure stop at the corner of the transportation desk and look at us. I hurried along a little faster, Steve's long legs taking one step to my three. It wasn't the Colonel I wanted to avoid as much as it was George, actually. I glanced back again as we reached the sitting room door. George was still nowhere in sight.

I put my hand out to turn the knob. A door just along the hall past my room opened. I looked around. Mrs. Ridley had started out, and seeing us slip back inside again. I heard the door close quietly. I glanced up at Steve. Either he hadn't noticed her or he didn't know her. Not, of course, that it mattered, except that her action seemed a little curious— almost furtive, in fact, and vaguely disturbing, like an elusive breath of cold air in a warm room. I turned the knob, tapping lightly with my free hand, and opened the door.

Mrs. Chapman was at the table in front of the window. She pushed the drawer shut with an abrupt movement of her body. I saw her put something down on the table as she turned; and I could see there, sticking out just a little from behind the purple print of her dress, the blue-glinting butt of George Pelham's revolver. Mrs. Chapman was facing Steve Grant, halted just two steps across the threshold, her face set rigidly, her ice-blue eyes searching his with steady piercing scrutiny. I closed the door and turned the key in the lock, and waited . . . the sharp electric silence of the room vibrating along every nerve of my body.

Neither of them—the square, intractable-visaged old lady, the tall steel-taut man in the olive green uniform of the Park Service—moved a muscle or made a gesture to lessen the distance that divided them like an abyss slashed across the narrow room.

Then suddenly, as I stood there, my heart almost frozen, I saw Mrs. Chapman's grim stony face soften, her cold icicle eyes fill with tears. Her lips trembled, she raised her arms and held them out.

"Steve! My boy!" she whispered.

For an instant so long that it seemed eternity Steve Grant stood taut and rigid, and then he was across the room and in her outstretched arms, his head buried on that formidable granite bosom. The tears were streaming down Mrs. Chapman's cheeks. "—Why did you do it, Steve?" She rocked his head on her breast, her voice so tender I could scarcely believe my ears. "Thank God we've found you, Steve! My boy, my boy!"

I turned the key in the lock, opened the door, slipped out into the empty hall, closed the door softly and crept along to my room. I stood there in the dark looking out the window through the inky fringe of pines to the lake, glittering silver-surfaced in the white moonlight. I didn't, I realized, know actually very much more about Steve Grant than I'd known three hours ago . . . but in that brief time, and just because of the people who believed so steadfastly in him—Lisa, Dutch, Monty, Mrs. Chapman—he had been completely absolved in my mind from everything he seemed to have done in the past.

A knock at the door brought me sharply around. I said "Come in." The door opened, and my son, in his pajamas and striped dressing gown he'd outgrown since June stood, tousled-headed and bewildered, in the oblong of light from the hall.

"For cat's sake, mother!" he exclaimed. He felt for the switch, clicked the light on and closed the door. His face was almost comically perturbed, his eyes still blinking with sleep. "It's darn near midnight. Where've you been?"

"Nowhere, darling," I said.

He came over and sat down on the edge of my bed beside me.

"Say, mom," he said after a minute, staring down at the

hole in the toe of his slipper. "Is it true Cecily's going to marry that big heel?"

"If you mean George Pelham, it seems it is," I answered.

"And is it true that the guy they thought was dead has turned up?"

I nodded. "Who told you?"

"Lisa," he said. Then he added, "She says Cecily's still goofy about him, and he's goofy about her. Is that right?"

"I wouldn't know, darling," I said, "but I wouldn't be surprised."

"Well then, what the heck she wants to marry that dope for I can't figure out."

"It's just life, Bill," I said.

"It sounds screwy to me."

"It is. It gets screwier and screwier the older you get."

I was talking about life still, but Bill had a concrete mind.

"I wish somebody would take him out and not come back till they buried him," he said.

"Bill!" I exclaimed. "You mustn't talk like that!"

"Well, Lisa says——"

"I don't care what Lisa says!" I lowered my voice abruptly. Lisa's father was probably sitting in his Victorian nightshirt, his ears glued to the keyhole on the other side of our connecting door. "Lisa's very apt to say anything that comes into her head. Now you go to bed and don't think about it."

He gave me a dutiful peck on the side of the cheek and wandered dejectedly back to the door. He stood there, his head down, kicking the rug with the toe of his slipper, his back toward me.

"Mother," he said miserably, without looking back.

"Yes, Bill."

"Mother—you aren't going to marry Colonel Primrose, are you?"

I gasped . . . quite literally. "—Why, Bill!"

He looked up unhappily. "I heard old Sour Puss telling his blonde you were going to marry him in spite of hell and high tide, and he's always hanging around, and I . . . well, I guess he's all right, but Gosh, mother——"

He tried to grin, but it didn't work.

"Listen, Bill," I said. He came over and sat down beside me again. It was after one when he kissed me good-night again, and I stood in my door until I saw him close his own. As I started to close mine I saw Mrs. Chapman's open and Steve Grant come out. He stood a moment, looking across the hall at George's door. I never saw a face so pale or quite so grim.

Suddenly he took two swift steps across the corridor and stopped, his jaw set, the lines at the corners of his eyes contracted with cold menace. He raised his clenched fist to knock, and halted it half an inch from the painted wood panel. I saw him look up at the open transom. George's rhythmic peaceful snores droned through it, rising and falling like the distant hum of an airplane motor.

Steve Grant dropped his hands and stood there. Then he jerked his powerful frame around and strode off down the hall. A silence so profound that it was almost tangible swallowed his sharp tread and settled eerily in the empty halls. I pushed my door to and got ready for bed. My hands shook a little as I took off my shoes—whether for what George had escaped or what was still to come I didn't know.

9

I was waked the next morning about eight with the mad rush of so many feet in the corridor that I sat bolt upright in bed and grabbed for my dressing gown. The place couldn't be on fire, I thought, because I didn't hear any bells—or any bombs, though it sounded precisely like the evacuation of a whole metropolis. I got up and ran to the window, and drew a sharp relieved breath. It was just the evacuation of the tourists. A dozen great yellow buses were lined up along the drive, baggage enough for an army stretched endlessly along the platform.

I thought suddenly that I hadn't said good-by to Lisa, and the Ridleys were joining the general exodus. I looked at my watch. I have an abiding dislike of facing the world before breakfast, and after facing George and a dozen horses before it for the last week, I'd been looking forward to this very morning. Still, I had a very special feeling for Lisa. I started to the bathroom to run my tub. It was off the short narrow passage that connected my room and the Ridleys'. They hadn't, apparently, been moved out yet, for I could hear Mrs. Ridley's voice. And I stopped abruptly. It was high-pitched and almost hysterical.

"You complain because she isn't attractive to boys," she was saying. "You won't let her dress like other girls so she will be, and now that a boy does find her attractive you're furious. Why didn't you take her away this morning the way you planned? You can't stay here and not let her go out of the hotel."

Mr. Ridley's voice was sharper than I'd heard it before.

"I'm staying here because Mrs. Chapman is determined to break up your brother's engagement to Cecily, and I'm going to stop her. That's why we're staying. You ought to thank me instead of turning against me."

"I don't thank you!" Mrs. Ridley cried. "I don't want him to marry her, and you know it! I'll do everything I can to keep him from it!"

Alexander Ridley's voice was deadly, ominously calm. "My dear, you'll do nothing of the sort. What you *will* do is see that your daughter doesn't see or speak to that young scoundrel. Do you understand, my dear?"

I heard the door into the hall close quietly. Inside the room there was nothing but sharp motionless silence. I slipped back into my bedroom, closed the door and rang for my breakfast. When the Filipino boy brought it, there was a scribbled note, slightly spotted with jam, on the tray beside it.

"Mom," it said. "—Lisa and I have gone to White Lake where they had the forest fire with Monty. Don't tell her Dad. It's his day off. He's a ranger and a good guy. Look out for the Man in the Iron Mask. The blonde's taken him to the Fish Fry. Love, Bill."

I read it again. Mr. Ridley obviously wasn't taking a day off, and since he wasn't a ranger and definitely, I should say, not a good guy, I gathered it was Monty that Bill meant. It certainly cleared the decks, I thought. It left the Colonel without his man Friday and me without Lisa, but on the whole it seemed a very good thing. Matters were already sufficiently complicated without the young barging in and out, threatening to exterminate George in parts or in toto, whether they meant what they were saying or not. Furthermore, they might just as well be having some fun out of the trip.

I'd just finished dressing when there was a discreet tap on my door. The Filipino boy came in and picked up the tray. "The gentleman Colonel Primrose, she in Mis' Chapman's room. She say, you come please pretty soon?"

"Thank you," I said. He backed out of the door, bowing and smiling, precariously balancing the tray, one hand feeling for the knob. "—She say very much pretty soon, please?"

My heart sank into the pit of my stomach. It wasn't the first time the Colonel had sent me a peremptory command to appear very much pretty soon please, and nothing good had ever come of it. I put on my jacket and picked up my hat and gloves. Just what was coming I didn't know, but I had a fairly dismal idea. I locked the door and went down the hall. As far along as the eye could reach it was piled with the rumpled bed linen of the departed dudes.

I opened the door of Mrs. Chapman's sitting room and went in. Colonel Primrose, looking familiarly grim, was half-sitting against the table in front of the window. My heart, already low, took another sharp nose dive to my boots: he had two hotel telegraph blanks in his hand. Mrs. Chapman was sitting in an arm chair beside him, George and Mr. Ridley were on a wicker sofa against the wall. George's face had a strange shuttered expression on it, compounded of satisfaction and wariness under a light frosting of casual boredom.

It was the other people in the room that terrified me. Cecily, her face pale, chin up, hands gripped tightly behind her back, was standing against the frame of the closed door into her room, her amber-flecked eyes as dark as old mahogany fixed resolutely out the window. In a chair beside the door was a short dark-haired man in the uniform of the Park Service whom I'd never seen before. Beside him, standing erect, his chin out, his jaw tight, eyes narrowed a little and burning with cold passionate anger, was Steven Grant. He wasn't looking at Cecily or at George, but directly and squarely at Colonel Primrose.

"You know all these people except the Chief Ranger Mr. Rayburn, Mrs. Latham," Colonel Primrose said. The man in the chair beside Steve got part way up, said "How d'ye do," and sat down again. He was rather nice, I thought, with a shrewd kindly face, honest and straightforward, and not, I should have judged, very easily taken in by anything. Colonel Primrose nodded at a chair in the corner near Cecily, and I sat down.

"—You admit, of course, Mr. Grant, that you did allow the authorities to believe you were killed in a motor accident, and that you have been going under an assumed name?"

I had the idea, as Steve nodded, that this was a recapitulation for my benefit.

"But you refuse to state the reasons for what seems like very extraordinary conduct indeed."

"I do," Steve said curtly.

I felt Cecily's slim body stiffen. She flashed around, her eyes blazing, her small fists clenched tightly at her sides.

"I'll tell you why!" she cried passionately. "It was because he didn't want to marry me, and I refused to release him! That's why!"

Steve's lean face, already pale under its tan, turned a harder and tenser white as he took a step forward. Then he controlled himself with a determined effort.

"That isn't true, Cecily," he said quietly. "You know it isn't."

"I know it is!" she retorted hotly.

Colonel Primrose interposed. "I don't think this is getting us anywhere," he said equably. "I'm acting here with the Chief Ranger on behalf of the Department in Washington. They were informed by wire that a temporary ranger stationed at Thorofare was going under an assumed name. I have the original of the wire here."

He held it out.

"Do you recognize this, Mr. Pelham?"

I felt Cecily stiffen again, and heard a sharp little gasp as she turned a pair of startled eyes on George, her lips parted a little.

George took the blank, looked at it and frowned. I watched him a little breathlessly. He raised his eyebrows, and handed it back to Colonel Primrose.

"I certainly do not," he said calmly. "And that is *not* my signature. Anyone will tell you that who's ever seen it."

For a moment I was just too appalled to speak. I sat there staring at him, absolutely aghast. Steve's face relaxed to puzzled amazement. He looked at Mrs. Chapman. She was looking from me to George, her eyes disturbed but wary.

"It seems to me," Alexander Ridley said, very smoothly, "that somebody is childishly trying to put my brother-in-law in an extremely awkward—not to say dangerous—position, for reasons of their own."

He glanced at Mrs. Chapman, and reached over to Colonel Primrose. "—May I examine that, please, Colonel?"

He took his glasses from his breast pocket and held them on his nose, looking down at the blank.

"The printing of the message supports that, as well as the signature," he said judicially. He slipped his glasses back in his pocket and handed the form to the Colonel. I bent forward in my chair. It was definitely my turn to speak.

"It was——"

Colonel Primrose shot me a swift silencing glance. "Who is John Brice, Mr. Pelham?" he asked sharply, drowning out my voice before anyone else was aware I was trying to speak.

George looked at him for an instant.

"Brice?" he repeated, in a puzzled tone. "You mean the clerk we used to have in the office? That's the only John Brice I've ever heard of. Steve knew him better than I did."

Cecily's breath came in a quick little gasp again. She looked at Steve, her face as pale as old ivory.

"Where is Brice, Mr. Grant?" Colonel Primrose asked.

I had the sudden feeling that this was the question Steve Grant had been waiting for, and that he'd long ago given up dreading, knowing that some time he had to answer it. And that answering it now that it had come was more of a relief than he'd thought it could be.

"He's dead," he said quietly.

I felt Cecily's body relax. She leaned her head back against the door frame and closed her eyes.

"It was him or me," Steve said dispassionately. "He had a gun in my ribs. I ran the car into a telephone pole."

In the abrupt silence that met this steady matter-of-fact statement Cecily's voice came as cool and surface-calm as twilight.

"—You mean, you deliberately murdered him . . . so you could pretend you were dead and so he could never take the stand against you?"

Steve's jaw dropped. He stared at her almost stupidly, his face blank and uncomprehending.

"I never believed what they said," Cecily went on. She was still outwardly calm, but all the low-pitched velvet undertones of her voice were charged with anger. "But I see it all now."

She turned to George.

"I'm . . . I'm sorry I was so stupid, and so . . . blind."

She turned, blinded suddenly again, groping for the door knob, pushed the door open and fled into her room.

Steve took a quick step forward. "Cecily!" For a moment I thought he was going to smash through the door with his shoulder. But he turned abruptly then and stood staring at George Pelham across the room, his eyes narrowed and cold and dangerous.

"Look, my boyhood friend and companion," he said with a twisted smile, "just what the hell has been going on while I've been gone?"

George looked rather more uncomfortable for an instant than I should have thought possible. He recovered himself, and shrugged.

"Now you're back," he said coolly, "perhaps you'll be able to explain what *went* on. There are a lot of people would like to know. It's unfortunate Brice is dead, of course. And Mrs. Stuyvesant.—Or maybe not. You'll know more about that than anybody else."

For a moment there was an intent puzzled look in Steve's face. It changed into one of blank incredulity. Then his face flushed angrily.

"You dirty, double-crossing house rat," he said. He laughed suddenly. It was sharp and peculiarly mirthless, and it made my spine freeze. He turned to Colonel Primrose. "Was that in the telegram too, Colonel?"

"More or less implied, I assume," Colonel Primrose said. His black X-ray eyes rested steadily on Steve. "In another telegram—with the same signature—sent to the States Attorney of Mecklenburg County."

"That's just dandy," Steve said, with a sardonic grin. "You know, it's funny about you, George. I thought you were pretty damn anxious for me to be on my way the other night. You're a smart boy, but you're not smart enough."

He turned to the Chief Ranger, who had risen and was standing by the door.

"Okay, Chief. I'll come quietly."

At the door he looked around at George. "But I'm coming back, Pelham."

His voice was even, but I don't think anybody could mistake the deadly promise in it.

The Chief Ranger nodded to Colonel Primrose. He followed the two of them out into the hall, pulling the door to behind him. After a moment he came back.

"I'd like to have a few minutes with you, Mr. Pelham," he said pleasantly. "My room is just along the hall."

George got up and pressed his cigarette out. "I'd suggest you get in touch with Miss Chapman's father," he remarked. All his old urbanity was in force again. "He knows more about this than I do. I was following his orders in the investigation."

"I fancy you can leave that to us," Colonel Primrose replied—equally urbane, if not indeed a little more so.

Mr. Alexander Ridley waited until the two of them had gone. "If my brother-in-law has made an error in judgement, Mrs. Chapman," he said, magnanimously, "I'm sure he'll be the first to admit it. He has always been as devoted as a brother to Steven Grant."

"Cain cut Abel's throat, if I remember correctly," Mrs.

Chapman replied curtly. "Frankly, Mr. Ridley, the only thing that disturbed me is that my granddaughter has quietly lost what little mind she had. Only a person completely bereft of reason would act as she's acting now. I trust she'll recover hers shortly."

How vain that trust was couldn't have been demonstrated more instantly. Cecily's door opened. She stood there in a dark green hat and checked jacket, her face parchment pale, drawing on her pigskin gloves.

"Grandmother, I'm going to marry George today," she said calmly. "I've always known you were very cruel and heartless. I didn't think you'd be so to me."

She crossed the room. Mr. Ridley opened the door for her, followed her out into the hall and closed the door quietly behind him.

Mrs. Chapman stood motionless, her pale blue eyes under their white lashes fixed on the painted panel for a full minute. Then she sat down heavily in the wicker chair. After a moment she said, "Go now, please, Grace. I want to be alone."

I went. Cecily and Mr. Ridley were disappearing rapidly down the hall toward the lobby. I walked slowly back to my room. As I put the key in the lock the door beyond me opened quietly, and Mrs. Ridley slipped out into the hall. She came running toward me, her face almost terrible with anxiety and dread.

"What happened, Mrs. Latham?" she whispered frantically, clutching my arm.

"She's going to marry him," I said briefly, knowing it was that and nothing else she was interested in.

"Oh no, no!" she cried desperately. "She mustn't, she mustn't!"

"Why not?" I asked, as casually as I could.

"Oh, because! Because! Oh, don't you see? I so hoped she wouldn't! It means so much——"

She shrank back abruptly, her face suddenly grey, as if I'd betrayed her into an awful indiscretion—as indeed I suppose I had. She drew herself up with a kind of tremulous dignity. "I'm sorry, Mrs. Latham. Forgive me! I'm a little upset, and Lisa's gone off with someone, and it annoys her father so. I——"

"She's probably having a lively time," I said cheerfully. "My son's along. He's a grand chaperon."

She backed away toward her room, and I went into mine. One of the odd things about Yellowstone—though I suppose, as I'd overheard Mr. Alexander Ridley pointing out, it isn't so odd when you consider that half a million people go around the Grand Loop from June to September every year —is the way you run into people you haven't seen since you graduated from the Primary Department. At lunch I met a woman I hadn't thought of or heard of since we were brides-maids at St. Bartholomew's and she stepped on the bride's train and ripped it. Her husband, it appeared, was out fish-ing, and her chauffeur could just as well drive the two of us to see the Grand Canyon. As I couldn't think of anything else, I said I'd go. We were crossing the lobby to set out when a bellboy came up to me, winking in the most friendly and informal fashion.

"Aren't you going to the wedding?" he grinned.

"Wedding?" I repeated stupidly.

"Oh, maybe it's a secret!" he beamed. "Mr. Ridley was asking where they could get a license, and he and Miss Chap-man and Mr. Pelham just left in the red car."

"Isn't that lovely!" I said. I tried to smile. Actually I could have slain Colonel Primrose. For some odd reason that was certainly without any foundation at all, I'd been so sure he'd prevent it that I hadn't really worried about it. I'd thought he would have George in some kind of technical—or un-technical—protective custody, or something, that would at least give Cecily a chance to come to her senses.

We'd started for the portico when suddenly I saw him through the door. I hurried along, opening my mouth to call him, when he stepped into the Chief Ranger's car. The bellboy out there slammed the door shut, and they shot off down the drive without a backward glance. My friend's chauffeur pulled in where they'd been, and we got in.

"Now, my dear, I do hope you aren't one of those awful people that likes to get out and climb over rocks and water-falls," my friend said, settling back comfortably. "I'm sure we can see everything from the road. I understand there isn't very much here anyway. I mean, except Nature. Now, my dear, tell me whatever made Philip marry that incredible young woman. Hasn't she a slight impediment in her speech . . . ?"

Whatever my old school friend conceivably might have had, it certainly was not an impediment of *her* speech. When we got back to Lake Hotel that evening, while I hadn't seen a waterfall I'd definitely experienced one, and I tottered into the lounge and sat down, completely exhausted. The bellboy, whom I seemed to have got on the most extraordinary terms of rapprochement with, came sidling over and bent down.

"They're coming!" he whispered.

"Who?" I said.

"You know!"

He didn't nudge me, but he might as well have.

I thought, "Oh, dear!" and got up quickly. Through the door I saw the big red car in a cloud of dust in the back courtyard. I picked up my hat and bag. I couldn't, no matter what happened, be the first to congratulate them. I hurried out of the lounge along the hall to my room and went in. I didn't turn on the light. The darkness and silence were like a heavenly benediction after all I'd been through, and I sat down and closed my eyes.

Suddenly I straightened up. There were quick running steps in the hall. They became louder and more sharply staccato, and stopped suddenly at Cecily's door next to mine. I heard the fumbling of the key in the lock, the door open and slam shut, and the agonized creak of springs as she threw herself down on her bed.

I got up and went to the door that joined our rooms. The muffled sound of aching strangled sobs came through the thin partition. I put my hand on the knob, and hesitated. Then suddenly I couldn't bear it another instant—it was too heart-breaking. I opened the door and went in. The room was dark. In the faint early glow of the moon from the lake I could see her forlorn little figure, huddled wretchedly on the bed, her face buried in the pillows.

I crossed the room and put my hand on her quivering convulsive shoulder. "Cecily, darling! What is it?"

She shook her head stormily in the pillows. "Nothing!"

There was certainly nothing forlorn or pathetic about her voice. It was choked with sobs, but they sounded more like wrath and defeat than anything else.

"I . . . I wanted to marry George—but they . . . they wouldn't let us out of the . . . the damn Park!"

She didn't raise her head—and I was glad she didn't, because I was grinning like the village idiot. I was thinking how I'd love to have seen George and the bland and confident Mr. Ridley . . . undoubtedly at the present moment wiring influential friends in Washington to have a dozen rangers fired.

I looked up quickly. The door from her grandmother's room had opened silently. In the yellow oblong of light I saw the grim old lady, in an incredible pink and green flowered negligée, supporting herself with her hand against the edge of the door.

"You mean then you *aren't* married," I said.

Cecily shook her head in the pillows again.

"No! They wouldn't let us past the gate!"

Mrs. Chapman closed the door softly. I heard the wicker chair creak as she sat down heavily inside her own room. I knew she was going through the same paralyzing relief I'd gone through the afternoon before, as I'd looked back over the long blue stretch of the lake to the hazy outline of the southeast arm toward Thorofare.

And with as little prophetic insight. For it was just two hours later that Mrs. Alexander Ridley stumbled over George Pelham's body, with a gunshot in the forehead, not fifty yards from the trailer camp in the pine woods.

10

But when I was there in the dark room with Cecily, George Pelham still had two hours to live. He was killed at twenty minutes past ten. His sister found him at half-past eleven. The twenty minutes past ten was definite and settled fact. The District Ranger himself heard the shot from his quarters, and remembered looking at the clock over his sofa. The people asleep in their trailers who heard it too assumed it was a car backfiring. The District Ranger knew it was a shot, but assumed it was being fired at the bear who'd been raiding the trailer camp and had had a death sentence passed on him that morning—he'd torn the arm practically off a woman who denied she'd been feeding him in spite of the fact that her hand was still sticky with candy.

The bear, however, by twenty minutes past ten had been dead over an hour, killed in the CCC camp behind the government mess and carted off to the incinerator, just while the District Ranger was off to the East Entrance to pick up a man who had three hundred and seventy-three cutthroat trout instead of his allotted five in the back of his car, headed for the fish markets of Cody. And as for George, no one seemed to know where George had been, after he and Mr. Alexander Ridley and Cecily had come in from their abortive trip to the North Gate and before Mrs. Ridley found him huddled in the pine woods behind the trailer camp.

It was a few moments before eight when Mrs. Chapman

had closed the door quietly on Cecily and me, more relieved, I suppose, than anyone could imagine that that trip had been abortive. Cecily sat up abruptly, her feet curled under her on the bed, and pushed her short damp curls back from her forehead. Her rage was easy enough to understand, heaven knows, even without that red hair and proud sensitive face. I suppose there's nothing that makes a woman, however young or old, so furious as to be prevented from doing something she knows in her heart is foolish, and that she's hell-bent on doing just because she's proud and her pride has been unbearably hurt. I think Cecily did know in her heart that she'd been hot-headed and impulsive in spite of her outward calm when she left her grandmother's sitting room. Maybe she hadn't consciously wanted to strike out and wound the people who had wounded her the most—Steve chiefly, of course, but her grandmother too, for what must have seemed the base treachery of taking him back to her simple if stony bosom as if nothing had ever happened at all.

Anyway, she sat there on the foot of the bed, almost poignantly young, her eyes hot and resentful, her face stormy.

"Grandmother thinks she can keep me from marrying George by having them close the Park gates, but she can't!" she said turbulently. "I've always treated him miserably, because I never believed Steve was . . . was like that. He's always been so sweet to me, and never said half the things he suspected, because he didn't want to make me unhappier than I was. I've been a complete fool—eating my heart out for a man that just walked out on me and didn't have courage enough to tell me so."

"Oh, darling!" I said. "—Are you sure?"

"Sure!" she repeated. "How could I not be sure, after everything that's happened? Grandmother just doesn't know. —Listen. For a couple of months Steve acted in the oddest way. He was unhappy and despondent. He kept sort of saying I mustn't feel I had to marry him just because I'd promised to, and all that sort of thing. I mustn't think it would be letting him down, and so on. I thought he meant because he'd been so ill and he was sensitive about it—because I *adored* him, Grace—you've no idea!"

Her lips trembled. She pressed them together like an angry child determined not to cry.

"And then that Sunday night he came down. I hadn't seen him for a week. George had been down twice. He said Steve had gone sort of . . . sort of loco. And then he turned up and said—well, he said it all over again. I tried to make him see I wasn't marrying him because I felt sorry for him, and then I got . . . I got angry. I said if that's the way he felt about it, and . . . oh, you know all the things you say and you don't mean."

She turned her head away, batting her long lashes to keep back the stinging tears.

"He went away. And the next morning I . . . I thought he'd run into the telephone pole because . . . oh, because I'd been so sure I was right, at first, and wrong to lose my temper—and it was my fault."

"Don't you think maybe you still were, and maybe that's the reason it seemed better if he was out of the way?" I asked gently.

"No," she said, flatly. At times she was certainly a chip off the old block in the next room. Her eyes blazed again through the tears still clinging to her dark lashes. "I certainly don't. Not when it was John Brice in the car. Not when he was gambling in the market with a client's money, and trying to make it look as if poor Brice was doing it. Mr. Ridley says it looks like plain unadulterated murder to him, and I'm not sure he's not right!"

"Rot," I said frankly.

She untangled her slim elegant legs and swung her feet over the side of the bed. The trembling appealing girl that was the Cecily who'd been in love with Steve Grant was back again, under the crisp cool exterior of a Cecily who wasn't going to let anyone see how hurt she was.

"You sound exactly like grandmother," she said evenly. She went over and switched on the light, picked up her feather puff from the dresser and batted her straight little nose with it.

"I at least make more sense than Mr. Ridley—who's certainly what one might call a special pleader in this case," I remarked.

"You're wrong about that, Grace," she said. "He tried to persuade us not to go to Gardiner today."

I thought skeptically, "Oh yeah?" But I didn't say it. Sweet reasonableness was not one of Cecily's more noticeable traits, just then, and tact has never been one of mine.

"And I'm going to bed. I'm going to marry George tomorrow if it's the last thing I ever do."

"Okay, my lamb," I said sweetly. "It's definitely your privilege, and your problem. You're certainly old enough to know your own mind. Only it would be funny if maybe your first instinct had been right, and Steve isn't as black as sin after all—and you didn't find it out until too late. Good night."

She stood there like a brightly colored balloon suddenly a little deflated. Her hands dropped to her side, her lips trembled again. Then the tempest brewed back into her eyes. There was no doubt in my mind that no matter how many times that struggle teeter-tottered back and forth, pride—and George Pelham—would win. She wouldn't have been human otherwise, I suppose, and that's what she was—vibrantly, passionately so . . . like the grim square old lady on the other side of the door, and like the man who had barged back from the dead, headlong into the only lives that mattered.

I went back to my own room. There was a light under the Ridley's door. I could hear Alexander Ridley's voice, and I listened shamelessly, without a twinge of conscience.

"You mean to tell you don't know where your daughter is, at this time of night, my dear?" he was saying, with that cozy, domestic warmth that I imagine characterizes the home life of a nest of cobras. "Then all I can say is, you'll go out and find her. At once, Mrs. Ridley.—Do you hear, my dear?"

"Alexander—she's perfectly safe. That young boy is with her."

Mrs. Ridley's voice was as near as the cracking point as a human voice could be and not smash into bits.

"My dear," her husband answered coolly. "You know nothing about that boy. He's supposed to come of a good family, but it was his mother who signed your brother's name to an incriminating telegram your brother never sent. Frankly, I wouldn't trust that woman—or her son—an inch further than I could see either of them. No one can tell me she wasn't behind that ridiculous performance at the North Gate this afternoon—she and her friend the Colonel."

"Then more power to them!" Mrs. Ridley cried passionately—something of her daughter breaking through her timorous passivity.

There was a long silence. He'd probably strangled her, I thought. Then I realized that in a sense it was the other way around; it was Mr. Ridley who was shocked speechless.

"My dear!" he said at last. "You haven't returned to that attitude?"

His voice was not so bland as it usually was.

"Listen, May. I'm not accustomed to being disobeyed. Nor

am I in the habit of making threats I don't carry out—as you know. And I'm telling you if anything happens to spoil this set-up, it will go hard with you, my dear, and harder with your daughter. Is that clear? Because I want it very clear indeed."

I could almost imagine the poor woman cowering against the end of the brass bed, completely terrified. I know I should have been. There was something—it's not too much to say something malignant—in the icy resolution in Mr. Ridley's voice.

"But . . . Alexander!" she cried desperately. "I haven't done anything to prevent it! I haven't! Truly I haven't!"

"Very well, my dear. And see you do something to help it. Try to make yourself a little more attractive—if it's not impossible. And tell your daughter what I've said."

"Why do you keep calling her *my* daughter?" Mrs. Ridley cried suddenly. "She's your daughter too! Oh, I know—you hate her because you've never broken her spirit! That's why you hate her! That's why you want——"

"My dear!"

Mr. Ridley's voice was like a cat-of-nine-tails across her frantic lips.

"That's enough. Go and find her. Bring her here to me."

"No!" Mrs. Ridley cried. "Never! You shan't——"

"Go and find her, my dear, and bring her here. I'll wait until you do. Hand me the book on wild flowers, please. Thank you. Every moment I wait, my dear, will be less pleasant in the end. Close the door quietly, please. Thank you."

I heard Mrs. Ridley's footsteps weave drunkenly along the corridor, going faster and faster until they were lost on the thick carpet. I was boiling with anger. How she could resist putting arsenic in his soup I couldn't for the life of me imagine. I picked up my coat. Mr. Ridley's chair creaked comfortably, a radio broke into gay lilting dance music. I closed my door noiselessly and hurried down stairs. I couldn't bear being in the room next to him.

As I passed the desk the mail clerk leaned out.

"Here's a note for you, Mrs. Latham. Lovely evening, isn't it?"

I nodded brightly. I suppose it was, although I hadn't had much time to notice. He took the note out of my letter box and handed it to me. It had that slightly grubby look that characterizes all my son's correspondence.

"Mom," it said. "Lisa and I and Monty are going to the

loge to dance. It's dead as heck here and Monty says there are a lot of kids over there and anyway Lisa's old man wont let her dance. Come over if you can shake the Army. Love, Bill.

"P. S. By the way can you lend me a dollar ($1) till pay day? Bill.

"P. P. S. We met Steve. He's okay. *Gee,* is he out to smear Georgie! O Boy! Bill."

I folded the note and glanced up. The Army—at least the portion of it that Bill had in mind—was coming toward me from the other side of the tub of oleander. It was very odd, seeing him without his monumental backdrop, these days. I'd got so accustomed to their twin image, the massive granite figure of Sergeant Buck respectfully to the rear of his Colonel but towering above and protruding on either side, that it still registered on my retina, and now it took me at least an instant to recognize that the farther outline was incorporeal.

"Good evening," I said. "Where's my old friend and well-wisher this evening?"

"He's gone to West Yellowstone to take in the night life, damn him," Colonel Primrose said. "He and his lady friend. I've needed him all day."

"What for?" I demanded quickly.

He looked at me with a quiet smile.

"To help get you out of the mess you got yourself in last night, by signing Pelham's name to the telegrams, for one thing."

"Well, he did write them," I said warmly.

"But he *didn't* sign them."

"I suppose it was pretty stupid." I was a little penitent—but not very much, I'm afraid.

"That's probably one of your greatest understatements, my dear," he remarked affably. "Fortunately the District Ranger had already notified the Superintendent and the Chief Ranger that Sam Graham was Steven Grant. The Secretary's wire this morning didn't come as a shock to anybody. Pelham—very foolishly, I think—is trying to deny the whole business. Cecily's the only person who believes him, but since she's the only person who counts so far as he's concerned, it doesn't get anybody anywhere."

"Did you stop the marriage?" I demanded.

"The Chief Ranger stopped Pelham. Cecily and Ridley were at liberty to go anywhere they liked."

His voice couldn't have been suaver.

"As I told Mrs. Chapman, he can't be stopped indefinitely.

Personally, I don't see that it isn't just prolonging the agony. Cecily's pretty headstrong. I don't think anybody seems to realize what a jolt she's had. Pelham's making the most of it —with his brother-in-law's able assistance. Just off-hand, I'd say there's a much greater family resemblance between those two than between Pelham and his sister."

"I don't see how she endures him!" I said hotly.

Colonel Primrose looked at me. "Force of habit. I learn from those young people in the trailer that her father ruled his wife and daughters with an iron hand. George took over, with the aid of a doting doormat for a mother, and Ridley's just continuing a tradition.—Of course, I must admit I don't have a great deal of sympathy for invertebrates."

"But you should hear him talk to her!" I protested. "They have the room next to mine. He's awful! She's terrified of him. He says the most cruel things to her—and he's as smooth as molasses."

Colonel Primrose smiled, but it was my torridity he was smiling at, not the Ridleys' python and rabbit private life as viewed through hotel keyholes.

"Well," he said, "let's get out of here for a while. You're not planning any more wars of chivalry, at the moment, are you? Because don't, not until we've got a truce in this one."

"I was going over to the Lodge," I said. "But—" I handed him Bill's note. I thought he'd be amused. But he wasn't. Then I remembered the last line about George getting smeared, and wished I hadn't.

He didn't, however, seem disturbed by that. He said, "Your son doesn't like me, does he?"

"No more than Sergeant Buck likes me, I imagine," I said. "Or than you like the glamorous Pearl. As a matter of fact he says he guesses you're all right, but Gosh, mother. That's more magnanimous than the Sergeant is—or than you are . . . about Pearl."

Then I wished I hadn't said any of that either, so I added quickly, to make it worse, "You aren't really disturbed about Buck and lady, are you?"

"I am, frankly," he said, more soberly than I'd ever heard him speak about his personal life before. "I met Buck out here thirty years ago. He was a private, I was just out of West Point. We were detailed to Pelican Creek to see about a buffalo herd and a gang of poachers. I got in front of the wrong end of a big bull. Buck rigged up a sled on a pair of skis and dragged me in to Mammoth—over fifty miles, at twenty-five below zero. He's saved my life a dozen times since—in the Philippines, in France. He could have retired twenty times on money made gambling, but he's gone along. He's done all the dirty work. We've divided the swag when there was any, but I've got all the credit. Most of it belongs to him. I just don't want to see him picked off by anybody like Pearl, that's all. Now let's forget it. Shall we go somewhere? The Lodge, if your son won't mind too much."

I hadn't realized, I think, just how strong the ties were between Colonel Primrose and his iron guard. I felt very guilty, because if it hadn't been that Buck regarded me— however erroneously—as a triple threat to their alliance, I doubt if he'd ever have come into Pearl's sphere of influence.

Colonel Primrose held my coat while I put it on. After the sticky hot summer nights in Washington the cold mountain air of Yellowstone was vastly pleasant. We went out and walked down to the lake.

"Tell me about Steve," I said, after we'd stood there looking out over the three hundred miles of dark undulating shore line, like the rim of a tremendous saucer filled full with shimmering quicksilver.

"He's not saying anything. In fact, he's so sore, and so bowled over by the whole business that he's not using his head."

"Is he under arrest?"

Colonel Primrose shook his head. "He's off duty. I must say the Park people are acting less like brass-hatted bureaucrats than any government department it's ever been my job to work with. They're an intelligent, levelheaded decent lot of people. They're behind him to a man, by the way. They don't take anybody till they know he's got the stuff—and this life takes plenty."

"They think Steve's a good man?"

"A damned good one. He's what they call an E. F. A.— Emergency Field Appointment. He refused it at first—said he'd rather stay as lookout on Pelican Cone. They didn't understand it, because it was a definite leg up. When he found out he'd be put out in the wilderness area at Thorofare he changed his mind. It's clear now, of course, he wanted to be as remote from people who might recognize him as possible. He wouldn't file application to be a permanent Ranger. That's under Civil Service, and they go through their past with a fine-tooth comb and a microscope. He probably figured he could get away with a fictitious personal history until the end of the summer as an emergency temporary appointment before Washington got around to checking details."

"He wasn't planning to stay, then?" I asked.

"Just a breather, I imagine," Colonel Primrose said. "—Buried alone on top of a mountain all summer and isolated just as much the rest of the year as winter keeper at one of the lodges. I suppose nobody'll ever know what a heartbreaking haul it was."

We'd walked along the side of the road past the store toward the Ranger Station. It was closed and dark except for the chinks of light through the curtains in the District Ranger's living quarters where I met Steve the night before. As we came up, the door opened and Steve came out. He was still in uniform. He stood for a moment, took out his watch and looked at it, put it back in his pocket, lighted a cigarette and strode off in the direction of the trailer camp. I looked at my own watch. It was a little after half-past nine. Colonel Primrose's eyes were following Steve Grant's tall straight figure through the naked pines.

"You know, it's a funny thing about the business of the check," I observed. "Night before last George was telling Cecily that if she didn't believe him she could see old Mrs. Stuyvesant. This morning he told Steve it was unfortunate she was dead."

I assumed he'd know perfectly what I was talking about, and apparently he did.

"Steve wired this morning," he said. "She is dead. She's been dead two years. He'd never heard about it, of course, out in the wilderness."

"Was she dead when George first told Cecily about it?" I asked quickly.

"I shouldn't be surprised. However, there's Cecily's father. . . . when we can get in touch with him. He's somewhere along the Gaspé Peninsula fishing, at the moment. When Steve got the wire from the Stuyvesant estate this morning, he shut up like an oyster. All he'd say was that anything he said with Brice dead too would make him look like a Boy Scout, and the hell with it. All he had was his word against George's, and he didn't expect anybody to believe anything he said."

We'd passed the Station and cut up the narrow road through the trees to a small open meadow toward the Lodge. As our path intersected the road that runs from the back courtyard of the Hotel up to the Lodge behind the trailer camp, Mrs. Chapman's big touring car shot past us. Through the cloud of dust it raised I could see her own square white-haired figure at the wheel. Steve Grant was in the seat beside her. Where they were going I hadn't an idea, of course —but they were going somewhere, fast.

11

When the dust in front of us subsided, we crossed the road and went up to the wide hewn-log rustic portico. From inside came the low swinging wail of a saxophone. Through the windows at the end of the porch I could see a lot of young people dancing. I couldn't see Bill at first, but I did see the two youngsters from the trailer camp, Dick and Barbara Winston. Colonel Primrose dropped his cigar and stepped on it.

"Excuse me just a minute—I want to go and phone," he said. "I'll be right back."

I sat down on the deserted porch, pleasantly dark and peaceful in contrast to the brilliantly illuminated hotel I'd come from, and watched the moon on the water. Suddenly the Lodge door swung open. I glanced around. Lisa Ridley and her mother came out, Mrs. Ridley obviously controlling herself desperately, her face in the dim slanting light through the windows haggard and drawn. Lisa's face was pale too, under her dusky mop of sooty black hair, but not haggard. There was more fire in every line of her body than I'd seen before.

Whether they couldn't see me in the shadow of the great log pillars of the porch, or whether they were so concentrated on their own problem, I don't know. They were certainly unaware that anybody else was there.

Mrs. Ridley's voice came in sharp breathless gusts. "Lisa —listen to me! You're not to go back to the hotel tonight. You're to stay with Barbara and Dick. Do you understand me? You're *never* to go back where your father is again."

"If you go back, mother, I'm going!" the girl retorted hotly.

"I'm . . . I'm not going back either—only tonight," Mrs. Ridley said desperately. "I'll get some of our things. We'll get Dick and Barbara to take us . . . oh, I don't know —somewhere—anywhere."

Lisa's voice was suddenly calm and practical. "Mother— we haven't any money, either of us. Barbara and Dick are on a shoestring."

"I know. But I'll—arrange, someway. I'll—I'll do something . . ."

"Look, dearest." Lisa put her arm around her mother's quivering shoulders, speaking gently as if she were talking to an hysterical child. "You go down to the trailer and lie down a while. I'll come as soon as I can without it looking crazy. We'll talk about it."

"No!" Mrs. Ridley said. "No, Lisa! You don't understand! They were nearly married today. And I've talked to George —he's perfectly ruthless about the whole thing. No, Lisa— there's nothing to talk about, nothing we can do, I tell you! And I've got to get back to your father. He's waiting. He's angrier than I've ever seen him. It's because he thought he'd outwitted Mrs. Chapman and they made a fool of him at the gate. But tomorrow they won't. Oh, you just don't understand it, Lisa. He hates us both. I never really believed it till tonight. Go back now, dear—I'll come in the morning."

"No, mother," Lisa said quietly. "If you go back now, I'll go too."

"Oh, you shan't!" Mrs. Ridley cried. "It's too . . . too degrading!"

"Then promise me you'll go over to the trailer, and wait till I come," Lisa said calmly. "I'll bring Barbara and Dick. Barbara's pretty sore about this too. Dick pretends he knew it was going to happen—but it would wreck all their plans too. Now please, dear. Go down and wait quietly, and don't worry. *Something* will happen—God wouldn't let it not!"

Her voice broke in a quick sob. She buried her head on her mother's shoulder for an instant, then raised it quickly. "You're *so* nice, mother—why do you have to have such an awful . . . family?—Please, go quickly. Here comes Monty."

Her mother hurried off blindly into the night. Lisa turned and ran up the broad steps.

"Where've you been?" she laughed. "I've been hunting for you everywhere!"

"I've been sitting in front of the powder room waiting for you, you heel," Monty grinned back. "Where's my gun? Who's my rival?"

They ran back into the Lodge, and in a moment I saw the top of their heads trucking past the window.

I was trying to sort out, in my dazed and befuddled mind, the things Lisa and her mother had said. Somewhere inside the Lodge a clock struck ten. I looked back. Colonel Primrose was coming across the broad log-raftered room. I got up and went inside to meet him. Through the door of the dancing room I could see my son with a pert pretty little girl in a sea-green sweater and skirt. He saw me—and the Colonel—and raised his thumb behind his back, jerking it significantly toward the floor a couple of times. I turned away, hoping Colonel Primrose hadn't seen him. But he had, of course, and he smiled very good-naturedly.

"When I'm his stepfather I'll remember that," he remarked, taking my arm. "—I don't know whether you know it or not, but you haven't had any dinner."

I suppose that's why we didn't hear, some fifteen minutes later, the shot that killed George Pelham. We were in the fountain room. The dance music was blaring out at one end of the lounge, a radio roared out the latest news from abroad a few feet from our table. We sat there until after eleven. Colonel Primrose paid the bill then, and we went back into the main lounge. I waved good-by to my child. He and Monty were obviously haggling over a bright-eyed little blonde job in a white sweater and red skirt who was enjoying it immensely. Lisa I couldn't see, nor Barbara and Dick Winston. They'd probably gone back to the trailer, I thought. It seemed so horribly incongruous, some way, to think of them over there with all those youngsters, having a grand time . . . and Lisa's father waiting in his hotel room with a book about wild flowers—and Cecily wrestling in hers, wrestling with the devil of pride against the small wounded voice of outraged hope.

For a moment I thought of telling Colonel Primrose about the Ridleys, and then I didn't. I wasn't in the mood, definitely, for the amused tolerance with which he regards my passion for other people's problems. So we walked along the grassy edge of the road toward the back of the hotel in silence.

I had just said, "I wish they had some street lights out here," when he stopped abruptly and put his hand on my elbow. I stopped too. In the dim narrow ribbon of the road, where the moonlit sky showed through the little clearing in the dark belt of pine, I saw a woman run crazily out from the shadows, stop, turn first one way and then the other, run a few steps further, stop and run back. And as she disappeared for a moment into the shadows where I'd seen her come reeling out, suddenly through the blank silence of the night came the most blood-curdling shriek I've ever heard.

It echoed wave after wave through the trees, and it froze every nerve in my body. Then it came again, echoing and re-echoing in the night.

Colonel Primrose, beside me one instant, was a dozen yards ahead of me the next. I heard his running feet beating on the dusty surface of the road. I ran madly after him, stumbling in the deep car tracks. Then he stopped as abruptly as he'd started, and I could see the woman now, not clearly but clearly enough, in the filtered moon-glow from the lake, to recognize her even before I recognized her voice. She was standing there swaying, clutching her throat, pointing into the trees. I saw a quick yellow ball of light pounce on the dry needle-covered ground, and pounce again and rest on the dark huddled figure of a man lying face up, staring sightlessly into the night, a hideous gory snake coiling out of the hole in his forehead over the gory pine needles matted viscidly there already.

"It's my brother," Mrs. Ridley whispered. "It's George. He's dead. He . . . he must have been shot."

There was a ghastly moment, as the three of us stood there, when it seemed to me the heavens would crack under the horrible silence. Then, as if I'd been deaf and could hear again suddenly, there was a turmoil of running feet and shouting voices, and people came from everywhere, swarming like locusts. Some of them were still dressed, some pulling on coats or dressing gowns; women from the trailers in curling pins, men with eyes bloodshot from sleep.

I leaned back against a pine. Colonel Primrose's voice was like something out of a nightmare.

"Get back, all of you!" he said curtly. A woman reeled and fainted. I heard a man's voice saying "Sight of blood always makes her sick—funny, never affects me," like a crazy line in a crazy play. Someone else said, "Here come the Rangers." I looked around.

Half a dozen flash lights battered the slender naked pine trunks, crisscrossing like searchlights playing in a darkened sky. In the light I saw two tall olive green clad figures running through the trailer camp. One was the District Ranger, Dutch. The other was Steven Grant. They crashed through the gaping morbid fringe of onlookers and came to an abrupt halt.

I could see Steve's face thrown into sharp relief by the sudden movement of the light in Colonel Primrose's hand. If he had any emotion of shock or surprise or horror about the man lying there on the ground—the man he'd called his old boyhood friend and companion with so much twisted sardonic bitterness just twelve hours before—it wasn't visible to me in his hard jaw or steady dispassionate gaze. He would have been more moved, it seemed to me, if it had been a dead grizzly lying there. Though that wasn't fair, and I knew it the instant it popped into my head. The tight grim lines at the corners of his mouth, the tension in his rigid body, showed that he was moved. But there was no maudlin business that the fact of death—or murder—had wiped the slate clean of the menacing antagonism and angry contempt that he'd felt that morning.

I looked back at the inert body on the ground. There was nothing intrinsically noble or tragic about it, lying there in the center of the small dreadful druid circle, empty except for the shaken figure of Mrs. Ridley staring blankly in front of her. There was something macabre and ritualistic about it—the night, the dark naked pines, the huddled figures outside the circle; Mrs. Ridley, a withered terrified priestess, and her brother, a human sacrifice—on the altar of Necessity, it flashed incongruously into my mind.

Or was it incongruous? Her words came beating back into my ears. "I'll . . . I'll do something!" And I thought instantly, "No—it's not too easy. She wouldn't have done it this way." I looked down at the drying blood matted with pine needles. He'd been dead before she ran drunkenly out into the road. But not long—the trickle of blood from his temple was too mobile, his hand as the District Ranger lifted it fell back too limp, lay too inert on the ground.

"All you people clear out," Dutch said shortly. "Get back to your camps. Don't pick up any souvenirs."

I saw a woman with a chin strap and white streaks of cold cream around her eyes drop something on the ground as she backed away. Steve bent down, picked it up between his thumb and forefinger and handed it to Dutch. It was a woman's costume clip set with pale sapphires and small brilliants. It was caked with blood and stuck with dry pine needles like a ghastly magnet with iron filings. I saw Mrs. Ridley's eyes fasten on it, her chin sag a little. Her hand crept up to the front of her dark coat; her fingers groped numbly at the high V-neck of her print dress and dropped to her side. She moistened her grey lips, her body swaying again, and closed her eyes to hide the sudden biting terror in them.

I looked at Colonel Primrose. I knew from the way he wasn't looking at her that he'd been watching every move she made—and that he knew the blood-stained clip was hers.

The District Ranger laid it gingerly on the ground and wiped his hand on the seat of his trousers. "I guess we need some light around here, first thing."

"Shall I bring the patrol car?" Steve's quick clipped voice said.

Dutch nodded. "Bring my camera and the bulbs in the top drawer in my room. Phone Mammoth headquarters. And step on it."

I could hear Steve's running feet pounding the dry earth. The last of the campers disappeared toward the camp. Dutch turned to Colonel Primrose.

"This is more your line than mine," he said. "You'd better take over. I don't want to bungle anything—on account of him."

He moved his head toward Steve's vanished figure.

"The Chief Ranger said to call on you if we got in a jam. This is one hell of a jam if you ask me."

He looked down the road toward the Lodge. The lugubrious strains of "Yellowstone, Yellowstone, Skies so blue, Friends so true," were softly sugar-coating the silent night. He straightened up.

"Those kids'll be swarming out any minute. I'll go down and put somebody out to head 'em off."

He strode down the road as "Home Sweet Home" followed the savages' nostalgic summer theme song.

Colonel Primrose, balancing on one knee in the duff beside George Pelham's body, looked up at Mrs. Ridley.

"Where were you coming from just now?" he said quietly.

She looked at him stupidly. Her lips moved, but no sound came from them. Her hand wandered in a vague gesture toward the tree, and dropped limply at her side.

"Where had you been, Mrs. Ridley?"

She made a quick startled movement with her head. "From . . . I was coming from the hotel," she said breathlessly.

I could almost see Colonel Primrose's black eyes sharpen.

"Not from the Winstons' trailer, Mrs. Ridley?" His voice snapped like a firecracker. "—Let me give you a sound piece of advice. Tell the truth. It pays in the long run. You were at Barbara and Dick Winstons' trailer, weren't you?"

Mrs. Ridley nodded dumbly. Colonel Primrose got up.

"Mrs. Latham—take her back there, and keep her there till I come."

Mrs. Ridley moved back. "No!" she cried. "They . . . they've gone to bed. They'll all be asleep. I'll . . . I'll go back to the hotel."

I looked at the Colonel. I knew he'd caught the significance of that "all." I knew he was thinking, if not, more likely, had thought, minutes before, that it was strange Dick Winston—if not Barbara—hadn't come barging out with all the other trailerites. It seemed strange to me too, now I'd thought of it, and disturbing—more disturbing than I cared to admit.

"Very well," he said shortly. "Go to the hotel with her, Mrs. Latham. If Buck's back tell him I want him."

Sergeant Buck wasn't back. I looked breathlessly around—literally breathless, from trying to keep pace with Mrs. Ridley's alternately frantic running and reluctantly dragging progress along the dark uneven road. The lounge was empty except for the ubiquitous and infernally cheerful bell boys.

One of them bounded forward. "A pitcher of ice water, Mrs. Latham?"

I shook my head. The news of George hadn't apparently seeped this far through the night. Or possibly it had—nothing, I'm sure, short of the total annihilation of all human, animal and plant life would dim the blithe enthusiasm of a Yellowstone savage. It was like trying to live decorously in a kennel of spaniel pups.

I raced after Mrs. Ridley hurrying madly down the corridor. Why she was in such a frantic hurry to face her husband, who must have covered the wild flowers and be well into the volcanic structure of the Park by this time—and ready to erupt higher than Old Faithful—I hadn't an idea. Nor had she, apparently, for she faltered suddenly, half-way up the short stairway to our level.

I caught up with her and took hold of her arm. It was trembling so violently that I gripped it tightly to try to steady her. Her face was as gray as putty a century old.

She tried desperately to control herself.

"My husband will be . . . terribly . . . distressed!"

She groped for words that would cover up the fearful prospect in front of her. It was a bitter commentary on a human life—rather two human lives—that her uppermost emotion when she'd just come from stumbling over the murdered body of her only brother should be a paralyzing dread of facing her own husband.

I said, "Why don't you come to my room and stay all night? And tell him in the morning?"

She straightened up quickly and finished the other two steps.

"Oh no, I wouldn't dare!" she gasped. "I mean, I think it

91

wouldn't be best. No, thank you very much. It's very kind of you, but——"

We'd come to my door. She shrank back from the short distance that separated us from her own as if it was a burning pit.

"—Would you like me to come with you?" I asked . . . on an impulse that I bitterly rued the instant the words were out of my mouth. It showed too clearly, of course, how much I'd gleaned about the life she tried to conceal.

She clutched at it as if it had been a life-preserver I'd thrown out just as she sank for the third time. "Oh—*will* you?"

I thought, dismally, "Oh, *Lord!*" My heart sank—as if for the third time too—and there was nobody around with another life-preserver.

We moved along a little haltingly, both of us, to their door.

"Maybe he's gone to bed," I said hopefully.

"Oh no," she replied, and added quickly, "He never goes to bed till quite late."

She put her hand on the doorknob. I could hear her sharp intake of breath as she steeled herself. She turned the knob and opened the door. Alexander Ridley, his back to us, closed his book.

"You're *very* late, my dear," he said. The sinister calm of his voice froze my spine. "Come in—both of you—and close the door."

12

If I could possibly have turned tail and run, there's no doubt in my mind I'd have done it. But it was too late. He knew I was there. He got up slowly and turned, his eyes narrowed, his lips a cruel thin line. Then, as his eyes fell on me, his whole face changed incredibly, with lightning speed.

"Why, Mrs. Latham! This is . . . unexpected. Come in. My dear, why didn't you . . ."

He smiled genially at his wretched wife and pulled a chair out from the wall. I realized with an appalling shock that of course it was Lisa he meant by that "both of you"—not me.

Mrs. Ridley moistened her lips. Her breath came sharply.

"Alexander!" she said quickly. "Alexander . . . I've got very . . . very terrible news."

He put the chair in the clear space between a couple of open suitcases and smiled tolerantly.

"Don't tell me that Lisa's eloped with a ranger," he said, a little satirically, but not, I thought, without full awareness that the mention of her name would recall his unfulfilled orders to the unhappy woman by the dresser, struggling to retain what little composure she had.

"Sit down, won't you, Mrs. Latham," he said affably.

"Alexander!"

Mrs. Ridley gripped the edge of the bureau. "Listen . . . it's George!"

Mr. Ridley stopped, not abruptly at all, nor was there any visible effect on his own very admirable composure. Visible to me, that is. That there was, and that she'd recognized it, I saw in the sudden intenser pallor around her lips and the way her fingers tightened on the dresser.

"What about George, my dear?"

"He's dead!"

The words came out of her lips so sharply that they seemed to sting the air.

Alexander Ridley's jaw dropped. A slow deep flush spread over his face. He stood there, staring silently, then took a step toward her. She shrank back, her eyes as wild as a hunted animal's. I opened my mouth to scream, and swallowed it, thank heavens, before it was audible to any one but me.

"My poor dear May!" he said. His voice was unsteady with emotion—or with the effort of pretending it, I wouldn't know which. He put his hands on her shrinking terrified shoulders and kissed her forehead.

"No wonder you're unnerved, my dear."

She was weeping hysterically—and again I didn't know whether from sorrow, or from relief that he hadn't slain her on the spot. He turned to me.

"Thank you, Mrs. Latham," he said earnestly, "for coming with my wife. George is her only brother. She feels this very deeply."

He opened the door. "Good night."

I got to my room like a bat out of hell—though Sergeant Phineas T. Buck's friend Pearl told me later that that's a word no lady would use—and sank down on my bed, as unnerved as Mrs. Ridley if not as vocal about it. I'd done Mr. Ridley an injustice—whichever way I looked at it. Either he wasn't nearly so awful as I'd thought, or he was much worse.

And almost immediately I knew it was the latter. I heard his wife's voice in quick anguished alarm.

"Oh don't, Alexander—you're hurting my wrist! Please!"

His voice was cold and shaking with rage. "Where is he? What happened? Don't stand there like a stupid fool. Tell me, I say! Where is he?"

"Out in the road, behind the trailer camp," Mrs. Ridley gasped. "I found him. He's dead, he was shot! Oh, you're hurting me, Alexander!"

She gave a moan of relief, and I heard Mr. Ridley push back a chair and move across the room. He must have paced back and forth a dozen times. I heard his tread for several moments, punctuated by his wife's dry sobs.

"He didn't shoot himself?"

It was a question and statement both. There was a long silence. Then I heard his voice again, so deadly calm that it was shattering.

"May . . . you killed him, didn't you."

There was nothing but silence that I could hear, but she must have answered him some way. He said, "*My* wife—a murderess!" It sounded like something out of a dank moldered sepulchre . . . or a Broadway melodrama.

"I didn't! I didn't!" Mrs. Ridley cried then. Her voice was shaking and hysterical, and I knew she must be terrified almost out of her wits. "I didn't, Alexander!"

I heard his steps again. The closet door opened, a wire coat hanger rattled, the door closed.

"I'm going out there," he said. "Listen to me, May. Don't talk to anybody. Don't let that Latham woman in this room. Quit shaking, and go to bed."

He opened the door, and closed it again. I thought he'd gone, but he'd evidently come back into the room. "Listen, May.—Have you told any one you didn't want George to marry Cecily?"

"No!" she gasped.

"Are you sure? Think carefully. It's important."

His voice was more like that of a lawyer for the defense than a husband's.

"Oh, yes, I'm sure! I haven't talked to anybody."

"Not Mrs. Latham?"

"Oh, no."

"Very well. Now go to bed."

I heard the door close again, and his footsteps pass my door. I waited till they were out of hearing down the hall, and I waited a few moments longer. I could hear Mrs. Ridley moving about, and her shoe drop on the floor. She would never dare to leave him now, I thought, and it made me ill to think it.

I opened my door and stepped out into the hall. The watchman making his rounds glanced at me curiously and went on. I hurried past Cecily's door to Mrs. Chapman's sitting room, and stopped, a little surprised at seeing the slit of light under the door. There was no reason she shouldn't still be up, but it hadn't occurred to me that I shouldn't have to wake her out of sound sleep. I tapped on the door.

Her belligerent old voice when she said "Come in!" was like milk and honey after the two I'd been hearing. I opened the door and stopped short. Sitting on the sofa, like something out of a remote and long-forgotten and grotesque past, was Joe Anders, our wrangler-guide from Cinnabar to Thorofare, still in his dirty blue jeans, and dusty boots, his orange kerchief still around his neck.

"Oh," I said weakly. "Hello."

"Hullo, Mrs. Latham," he said, pulling himself to his feet. "How's Bill?"

"He's fine," I said.

Mrs. Chapman spoke brusquely. "Come in and sit down. And shut the door."

I hadn't realized I'd been standing stupidly half in and half out of the room. And why the information I'd come to bring her should suddenly have seemed like a large and heavy load of coals being brought to Newcastle I haven't an idea, but it did. I closed the door.

"If you'd like something to drink, help yourself," Mrs. Chapman said. "And sit down. We know about George. The night watchman told us."

She looked at me with a hard old eye. I don't know why I should have thought there was a challenge in it.

"It don't hurt my feelings," Joe Anders remarked calmly.

"Shut up," Mrs. Chapman said grimly. "They'll have you in the pen, first thing you know."

She turned to me. "—His sister found him?"

I nodded, got up and poured myself a glass of carbonated water. I didn't want it, but there was an uncomfortable strain in the room that made activity of any kind easier than just sitting.

Mrs. Chapman got up too. "I wish he'd come," she said irritably. "I hope that friend of yours hasn't put him in handcuffs. All policemen are fools."

She raised her head. "Maybe that's him. Look out there, Joe."

Joe Anders got up, his spurs clanking as he crossed the room and opened the door. He nodded back at her. I put down the bottle of soda and waited. I could hear heavy steps' —several pairs of them—in the corridor. In a moment Steve Grant appeared. He didn't have handcuffs on, but Colonel Primrose was behind him, and behind him was the short dark figure of the Chief Ranger.

Mrs. Chapman, who'd stepped forward to speak to Steve, stopped and sat down again, just giving them a short nod.

"Well," she said curtly, "we know Pelham is dead. Shot. You can get on with it from here. This is Mr. Anders—Colonel Primrose. And you two know each other."

The Chief Ranger nodded. I looked at Steve Grant. His eyes, in spite of him, I thought, had moved toward the closed white panel of Cecily's door. A sharp barb of pain stabbed through them as he turned away and sat down, the muscles of his jaw contracting in white ridges.

The Chief Ranger put his hand in his tunic pocket. "We're checking up on this, Mrs. Chapman," he said shortly. He pulled his hand out. In it was a revolver, its deadly blue steel irridescent in the lamplight.

I heard my own breath draw in sharply, and I tried to control it, because you could hear anything in that silent room.

Mrs. Chapman looked at the gun lying in the Chief Ranger's open palm, her face inflexibly calm and undisturbed.

"That's George Pelham's," she said. "I took it away from him on the other side of the lake. It's been here in my table drawer ever since."

"It was out in the huckleberries, half a dozen yards from where Pelham's body was found, a few minutes ago, Mrs. Chapman," the Chief Ranger said evenly.

"It was on my table the last time I saw it," Mrs. Chapman replied.

"It's against the Park regulations to have unsealed firearms in your possession, Mrs. Chapman. As you know."

"That gun was unsealed when it was handed to me, Mr. Rayburn," she said curtly. "The other gun in the party is still sealed."

"When was the last time you saw this gun, Mrs. Chapman?"

"I don't recall. It was here last night. I don't remember seeing it this morning. It may have been here."

I was looking at Steve Grant. His head was raised; he was staring straight ahead of him across the room, his face suddenly pale, his eyes almost desperate. I turned my head.

Cecily's door had opened so silently that not one of us except Steve had heard or seen it. She was standing there, her face above her white flannel dressing gown whiter by far than the flannel, her red-gold hair a halo of sleep-rumpled curls, her eyes dark amber wells. She was lovelier than I'd ever seen her, but quite terrible in a way too—like an avenging angel, almost, it seemed to me.

Her grandmother turned abruptly. So did the Chief Ranger and Colonel Primrose. Cecily's eyes were fixed on the blue glittering steel.

"My grandmother isn't telling the truth," she said, very quietly. "She knows that gun wasn't here this morning. She gave it to Steve Grant last night. I heard her say, 'Take this thing and have it sealed before somebody puts a hole in George Pelham's head.' "

The momentary silence that punctuated those last cool awful words was broken abruptly by her grandmother's grim voice.

"You're wrong, Cecily. I said, 'Take this damned thing and have it sealed before *I* put a hole in George Pelham's head.' —If you're going to repeat things you hear, repeat them accurately."

13

Whatever could be said for the thunderbolt with which Cecily so relentlessly shattered her grandmother's efforts to dissociate Steve and George Pelham's unsealed gun, one thing was very clear indeed. It shattered Cecily herself infinitely more than it did her grandmother. Long after the grim-faced little group in Mrs. Chapman's sitting room had broken up and I'd gone to bed, I could hear her in her room next to mine, toss and turn and get up, go back to bed and get up again, until I thought I'd go out of my mind too. Perhaps it should have occurred to me that it was grief for George Pelham—but it didn't, not even once.

And in the morning, just as I was finishing breakfast, she opened the door that separated our rooms and came in. She was fully dressed with her hat and checked jacket on, her cheeks tingling with the cold brisk early morning air, so I knew she'd been out for hours somewhere.

She pulled off her hat and sat on the side of my rumpled bed, her eyes fixed on the rug between her small dusty brown oxfords.

"He's gone," she said, without looking up.

I looked at her blankly. My heart sank. Steve Grant hadn't, when he left with the Chief Ranger and Colonel Primrose, been under arrest precisely, but he wasn't so far from it, it seemed to me, that he'd be able to say "Well, I've had enough of this, cheerio!" and walk off to California. And I couldn't believe he'd just bolted again. There was a jail at government headquarters in Mammoth, fifty miles away, somebody had told me. But that didn't seem to make much sense.

"I'm sorry about last night!" Cecily said dismally. "I . . . shouldn't have said what I did. I didn't mean to. I was just . . . just being cruel, to both of them."

"Something, certainly," I remarked.

"Oh, don't!"

She turned her head quickly.

"I know I was horrible, but I'd heard everything they said about George, and . . . well . . ."

She got up, went over to the window and stood looking out, her back to me, for a long time. Then she came back and sat down on my bed again.

"Anyway, I went over to the Ranger Station this morning to tell him I didn't mean it. But he wasn't there. Nobody was, except Monty. There's a forest fire beyond Pelican Cone and they've all gone."

"They'll be back," I said. I was more relieved than she knew. Just then it seemed to me that a fire, even if it spread over the entire 2,221,772 acres of Yellowstone Park, was preferable to Steve being in jail somewhere, or in flight.

"—But what . . . what if something happens to him?"

I looked at her suddenly anguished little face in complete surprise, and put down my coffee cup.

"Oh," I said.

"You don't understand, Grace!" she cried. "I . . . I just couldn't bear it!"

"No, I'm afraid I don't understand at all," I said, though I did perfectly. "Last night you were trying to hang him. This morning you're afraid he's going to get a cinder in his eye. Make up your mind, darling."

"I have made it up," she said calmly. She picked up her hat, went back to the door and turned around.

"George wasn't a very admirable person, in lots of ways,

but I don't think grandmother was right when she said that in twenty years I'd be just like Mrs. Ridley. If I married him. And maybe Steve did . . . shoot him. Only I think if he had he'd just have done it and not made any bones about it.—At least if it weren't for that Brice man," she added reluctantly. "I don't know how to explain that."

"Perhaps if you'd give Steve a chance, he could do it," I said patiently. "Unless, of course, he goes barging in and gets himself burnt up in the fire just because he doesn't give a hang anymore."

"You're trying to frighten me," she said. She turned quickly and went on into her room. I think I'd probably frightened myself as much or more, because I abandoned my breakfast at that point and got dressed hurriedly.

Mrs. Chapman had left her room when I went past, and the door of Joe Anders and Bill's room was open, a maid doing the beds more silently than usual. In the lounge I saw my son. He was making for the back door, busy as a bird dog. He saw me and dashed back.

"I'm going out to Squaw Lake with Joe," he said excitedly. "Say, who do you think bumped George off? He's in the dog house."

I looked at him aghast. "Bill!"

His face fell. "Well, that's what Monty said. That's what they call it. It's where they put guys that get drowned or . . . or run over. Colonel Primrose's over there now."

"Oh," I said. I was a little appalled at the enthusiasm with which he took the first violent death that had ever come his way. It was just another radio skit of cops and robbers, for all the reality it had to him. He looked at me.

"Oh, gee, Mom, I'm sorry. But a guy like that had it coming. He was trying to queer Steve and make it look like he was a crook. Joe says——."

"Listen, Bill," I said sharply. "You mustn't say such things! And above all, darling, *don't*, for heaven's sake, go around repeating what Joe or Lisa or Steve or Monty or *anybody* says now, or said at any time, about George. This is a serious business, sweetie-pie. Now go on with Joe, and stay away if you can bring yourself to it. The Colonel's very nice—but he's a policeman. He'd hang his own grandmother. Even Sergeant Buck says so."

Bill's face lighted up. I couldn't have done more to boost Colonel Primrose's stock if I'd done it deliberately. He grinned irrepressibly. "Just so he doesn't hang Cecily, it's okay with me, mom."

"He'd do that too," I said, but he was off.

I turned dejectedly. As a matter of fact, after last night it wouldn't have surprised me much if that was exactly what he had in mind. I picked up a newspaper somebody had left and sat down on a sofa in front of one of the broad clear windows looking out onto the lake, glittering and blue. I felt the springs creak and go down alarmingly, and looked up. Sergeant Buck's blonde friend smiled engagingly at me from the other end of the sofa.

"It's a lovely day, isn't it," she remarked.

"Yes," I said.

"I've been wanting to talk to you. You don't object, do you," she inquired politely.

She was watching me through a pair of very shrewd baby blue eyes, skilfully enlarged with blue eye shadow and mascara. I envy people who can use mascara. I smear it so that I look as if I'd been starved and ill for six months. She was smiling with that slightly complacent air of one woman who knows another's secret designs and is prepared to use them for barter and trade.

"Colonel Primrose is awfully busy this morning, isn't he?" she asked significantly. "Mr. Buck is on the case with him."

"They usually work together," I said.

"Mr. Buck doesn't have to work, does he?" she went on, casually.

I wanted to say he'd starve if he didn't, but I thought that would be a little transparent, Pearl doubtless already having a fair general inventory of Sergeant Buck's worldly goods. So I said, "Oh no. He's very rich, you know."

A satisfied little smile settled in one corner of her red mouth.

"No, I didn't. But then I don't think money counts very much. I think love is the important thing."

I let that one go. She served again.

"I should think Mr. Buck would want to set up for himself, now that he's so well fixed," she said. "Instead of being under somebody else all the time."

I thought of the Colonel's tribute the night before, but I didn't say anything about it. I just said, "It is odd, isn't it."

Pearl took a slightly soiled feather puff out of her elaborate vanity kit and powdered her nose thoughtfully. I took out my compact to powder mine, and dropped it. The whole thing came apart on the floor and I said, "Damn!"

She raised her plucked brows. "Mr. Buck doesn't think it's ladylike to swear."

"He's quite right," I said, gathering the pieces up and getting them together again, and getting a run in my stocking as I did it. "But he's rather uncompromising, you know."

"I don't think anything matters if you love a man," Pearl said. "Personally, I wouldn't think of marrying anybody just for their money."

Whether she didn't know what uncompromising meant, or just wanted to get on with her investigation, I didn't know. Anyway, I said, "I should think it would depend on how much he had."

She looked at me cautiously.

"How about Colonel Primrose?" she inquired, not very craftily.

"My *dear!*" I said. "He's poor as a church mouse."

"Then what——"

She caught herself abruptly and looked at me out of the corner of her eye. I pretended I hadn't heard her.

"It's too bad Sergeant Buck doesn't like me," I said. "Of course, *I* wish he'd marry and move away from Washington, so . . . well, I think a man is better off with a home of his own."

She smiled. "You mean, so you could marry the Colonel!"

I knew she was thinking it, but I hadn't expected her to say it, quite. I smiled. "Don't be silly. I wouldn't think of marrying again."

She gave me a skeptical sidelong glance.

"As a matter of fact," I said, glancing over my shoulder at the long empty lounge and lowering my voice discreetly. "Buck wouldn't be a bad catch, you know, even the way things are. Of course, the Colonel doesn't want him to marry. He'd have to pay a lot more income tax, because I suppose if Buck didn't work for him he'd transfer his property back, to his own name."

I felt the sofa springs go ping! and saw her shrewd blue eyes contract a little. I had dealt Sergeant Buck's economic status a frightful blow right in the solar plexus. Whichever of them was the church mouse now, it wasn't the Colonel. I got up.

"I do hope you're not leaving for a while," I said sweetly. "There are so many interesting things to do around here. If the Colonel doesn't need his car this evening, why don't you and Buck go down to watch them feed the grizzly bears?"

She looked at me, her eyes puckered at the corners. "—It's Mr. Buck's car, isn't it?"

It was, of course, as I knew very well. But having long

since abandoned the truth, there was no point in my returning to it at this moment.

"—Buck's car?" I repeated, permitting myself a faint smile. "If he told you so . . . of course it is. It certainly's registered in his name."

I laughed lightly. "Well, I'll probably see you around again. You haven't seen the Colonel this morning, have you?" Since she knew from Sergeant Buck that I was out to marry him in spite of hell and high tide, I thought I'd better add a little something to disguise my brazen pursuit to make her sure of it. "I must ask his advice. I'm having the most frightful time with my seventeen-year-old son. It's such a mistake, to marry as young as I did."

I went back through the long gay sun-lit lounge and glanced around. Pearl had lighted a cigarette and was sitting there, blowing very thoughtful feathers of smoke through her nostrils. I knew she was checking her—I suspect—rather extensive experience with the perfidy and deceitfulness of the male in pursuit of the female with an equally extensive and more first-hand experience of the scheming cupidity of the female in pursuit of the male. In any case, I thought, first blood was to me, definitely. My only fear was that if it got to the ears of Colonel Primrose's "functotum" I might as well, as he says himself, quit the country and climb a tree. But Pearl, I suspected, was too advanced for the direct approach —at least I hoped she was.

I turned the corner into the main lounge, and wished I'd stayed with Pearl a little longer. Colonel Primrose was at the transportation desk, and at the end of the corridor to our rooms I saw the large blond handsomely-tailored figure of Mr. Alexander Ridley bearing down on him. I started to dodge over to the news stand, but Colonel Primrose, who has eyes in the back of his head, turned and beckoned to me.

"Look," I said. "I've just been working on that fine figure of a woman who's working on your friend the Sergeant. Don't be surprised at anything you hear."

"I've known you too long for that," he said, with a left-handed smile. "But I want to talk to you."

"I don't know anything, about anything," I said positively. "And anyway here comes Mr. Ridley."

Alexander Ridley's face was troubled. He pulled up a chair in front of Colonel Primrose and me and sat down.

"My wife got your message, Colonel," he said. "She is not in any state to be badgered, I'm afraid. I'm trying to find a doctor for her without sending clear to Mammoth. She's terribly upset. George was her only brother. The bond between them——"

"I have no intention of badgering her, Mr. Ridley," Colonel Primrose said. "I'm only trying to collect information from any one who was around here last night."

Mr. Ridley nodded. "I can tell you all my wife knows. She went over to the Lodge last evening to watch the young people dance. Our nephew and niece Dick and Barbara Winston—charming youngsters—have a trailer in the camp below the Lodge. Mrs. Ridley hasn't been very fit recently—The altitude here affects her. She had a headache, left the Lodge and went down to the trailer to lie down for a moment and wait for Lisa. Personally, I think the child is old enough to have a little freedom, but you know how mothers are with an only daughter."

I listened to him virtually open-mouthed. He couldn't have been more wonderful!

"She lay down and dropped off to sleep. The children came over from the Lodge about eleven, and waked her. They persuaded her to allow Lisa to stay all night with them, and she started home about eleven-thirty. You know the rest."

I sat there, my eyes wide with admiration. If I hadn't heard all the same facts so differently stated, I should have believed every word of it. It sounded so natural and normal, the way things work in ordinary families.

"—And you, Mr. Ridley?" Colonel Primrose inquired.

"I was reading in my room. I came down and sent off a couple of wires, earlier in the evening, and I came down again for a scotch and soda a few minutes before eleven. I started to walk up to meet my wife, and daughter, after that, but I didn't have a flashlight. It was so dark I couldn't see very well, so I came back to my room."

My spine chilled. I could see Mr. Alexander Ridley setting out for those two people and changing his mind, thinking he could deal with them more thoroughly in what he considered the privacy of his room.

"When did you see Pelham last?"

"We dined together after we came in with Miss Chapman," Mr. Ridley said. "He stayed out here, talking to one of the young ladies of the orchestra. He said he was going out later to see Barbara and Dick. He didn't, obviously, or my wife would have seen him. Unless of course, he came before she left the dancing."

"You're sure she didn't see him?" Colonel Primrose asked.

"Oh, quite. I asked her particularly, and I have no reason to think she'd be other than perfectly frank."

Colonel Primrose nodded in entire agreement.

"How did Mrs. Ridley feel about her brother's marriage to Miss Chapman?"

Mr. Ridley hesitated. Then he spoke reluctantly, but not too reluctantly.

"Frankly, Colonel Primrose, she would have preferred he didn't marry at this time. As you'll easily discover—so that there's no use in not laying all the cards on the table at once —his marriage would make a very considerable difference in Lisa's situation."

Colonel Primrose's black X-ray eyes rested steadily on him. "How, Mr. Ridley?"

The large blond tailored man hesitated again, and then went ahead easily.

"My wife's father left his estate in trust to be divided in equal shares among his grandchildren," he said, "—when the youngest grandchild was twenty-one. Lisa is nineteen, and presumably would inherit a considerable sum in a year and a half. We have another married son, and my wife's sister has a son besides young Winston over at the trailer camp. If any of the three children—my wife, Mrs. Winston and George— had no offspring at the time of the division, and George presumably wouldn't have, he was to receive a merely nominal sum from the estate. That didn't affect George very much— he had a sizeable income from his mother, who left her entire fortune to him. I think he regarded it as a fair enough division of the spoils. I'm sure his decision to marry Miss Chapman at this time was in no way affected by any of these considerations. After all, he's been trying to marry her for several years. If he'd been interested in having a child to share in his father's estate, he would have married much earlier. Anyway, Miss Chapman is very comfortably off herself, as you know."

"If Mr. Pelham married, within a year and a half, in other words," Colonel Primrose said, "and had a child—as he undoubtedly would, to secure a share of his father's fortune— the division of the estate would be put off for another twenty-one years?"

"Precisely," Mr. Ridley said.

I was just plain staring at him, even though I remembered, now, what Mrs. Chapman had told me across the lake. Colonel Primrose put the question in my mind much more dispassionately than I could have put it.

"Weren't you—if I'm not mistaken, Mr. Ridley—rather aiding and abetting your brother-in-law in his plans for an immediate marriage?"

Mr. Alexander Ridley smiled.

"You don't imagine I'd seriously engage in a program that would keep my daughter from coming into an inheritance?" he asked, a little sardonically. "—But as a matter of fact, if George was determined to marry, Lisa didn't need money. I'm still able to take care of my family. Miss Chapman was a splendid match. I've met her father, though I've never had any business relations with him. Frankly, balancing the two things, I felt that a connection with the family would be a greater benefit to me personally, if I can be quite frank, than the division of the estate. But that's obviously not true from my daughter's point of view, and of course I wouldn't do anything to injure her.—So it certainly can't be said that I aided and abetted the proposed marriage, Colonel. On the contrary, if you'll ask Miss Chapman, she'll tell you that I tried to persuade them both from any precipitate action."

Mr. Ridley got up.

"That's the situation, Colonel. And now, if you'll excuse me, I'll return to my wife. If you see my daughter"—he gave us an affectionate smile—"will you tell her that she isn't twenty-one yet, and that her father misses her?"

He left. And I sat there practically on the boiling point. It's supposed to be much lower at this altitude, but I would have boiled if I'd been under sea-level.

"But that isn't true, Colonel Primrose!" I protested violently. "I mean about his not aiding and abetting the marriage. He's done everything he could!"

I told him the whole story—except about Mr. Ridley's calling his wife a murderess. I couldn't bring myself to that.

"I don't even mind having to confess I've been a dreadful eavesdropper," I said. "He's just doing it to hurt Lisa. I think he's terrible!"

Colonel Primrose looked at me with a maddening smile.

"Unfortunately, my dear," he said affably, "you can't hang fathers for cruelty to their offspring."

He shook his head. "It's unbelievable, isn't it. I thought they'd all died with Queen Victoria."

He reached in his pocket and took out a sheath of hotel

telegraph blanks. "These are the wires he was sending last night."

I read them. The top one was to his own office in the Banker Guarantee Building.

MAKE APPOINTMENT AFTER ELEVEN TOMORROW JOHN L CHAPMAN CHAPMAN AND DAVIS LUNCH SULGRAVE CLUB MONDAY IF POSSIBLE STOP PELHAM MARRYING HIS DAUGHTER STOP DONT MENTION BOYLESTON PROSPECTUS MAKE IT ENTIRELY PERSONAL FLYING BACK THURSDAY ALL SET THIS END

A RIDLEY

The next one was to a law firm in Cody, just outside the East entrance to the Park.

ARRANGE MARRIAGE LICENSE FOR GEORGE PELHAM AGE THIRTY-THREE AND CECILY CHAPMAN AGE TWENTY-THREE ADDRESS IN NEW YORK SOCIAL REGISTER STOP MARRIAGE TO TAKE PLACE TEN A M TOMORROW WEDNESDAY

ALEXANDER RIDLEY
RIDLEY AND HALL NEW YORK

The third was in the same handwriting, but signed "May Ridley." It was to a woman I'd heard of in New York who manages a lot of well-known coming-out parties. It read:

CANCEL ALL PLANS AND DRESSMAKER ARRANGEMENTS FOR LISAS PARTY STOP HER PROSPECTS HAVE UNFORTUNATELY CHANGED AND I AM MOVING HER TO THE COUNTRY FOR THE FUTURE

I read the three of them, completely furious.

"That shows he was trying to aid and abet the marriage, doesn't it?" I demanded hotly. "He was really trying his best to hurt his own child!"

Colonel Primrose nodded. "He just doesn't want the girl to have the means of freedom."

"And she got them in spite of him," I said.

He nodded again. "I'm very much afraid she did," he said slowly.

I looked at him—the significance of what he was saying, and of the way he said it, dawning on me with horror.

"Colonel Primrose! You can't—" I began breathlessly.

"Murder is murder, my dear," he said calmly. "I've told you that a good many times. The motive—or the excuse, rather—doesn't count. Not until it gets into court, anyway."

I started to speak again. He interrupted me very suavely.

"—I know all about it. There were a lot of people here who didn't mind seeing George Pelham dead. They're so frank in saying so—including, may I say, your own son—that it's a little disconcerting."

I didn't try to answer him.

He took an envelope out of his pocket, opened the flap and slid out the sapphire and diamond clip, still tarnished with dark dried stains between the jewels and in the spring fastener.

"I was going to ask Mrs. Ridley if this was hers," he said.

"You know it is," I said unpleasantly. "You saw her feel at her neck for it when she was saying it."

He looked at me without saying anything, sealed the envelope up again and put it back in his pocket. "Well," he said, "this will be one time when she'll have his whole-hearted support. It won't do him any good professionally to have her convicted of murder."

"His support in public, probably," I said. "God help her in private."

He got up. "What about some lunch?"

"I'll be back in a minute," I said. "I've got a run in my stocking."

He smiled. "I noticed you had."

14

In my room I could hear the Ridleys.

"I want you to stay in this afternoon," Mr. Ridley was saying. "I don't want Primrose to talk to you—do you understand? He's just like a ferret in a rat hole. And if I find a doctor, my dear, kindly continue to look unnerved. You do it well enough ordinarily."

Mrs. Ridley was apparently too unnerved at that moment to answer. And that, in some quite irrational way, increased my annoyance at Colonel Primrose. If Mrs. Ridley had murdered George as her husband seemed privately convinced, it seemed to me a thoroughly justifiable homicide, though why she hadn't picked her husband instead of George was a mystery to me. At lunch—and lunch at the Lake Hotel is something very special, the food's divine—I could hardly manage to be civil to the man who, if she hanged for it, would hang her. At least, I could hardly manage until I saw Pearl come in, in her bright pink slacks and a bright pink sweater. Then I instantly became so charming and beguiling that Colonel Primrose looked at me across his plate of cold turkey and jellied salmon and cucumber as if I'd lost my mind.

"Don't misunderstand me, Colonel Primrose," I said. "I just assured Pearl I'm not trying to marry you, and now I'm trying to convince her she understood me perfectly."

He chuckled.

"Go right ahead," he said agreeably. "I'm enjoying it, personally—as Pearl says."

"It's a little hard on me," I retorted. "I'm only doing it for Sergeant Buck. And where is he, by the way?"

His face sobered. "He's doing a little leg work. Checking up on a number of people. And asking a few discreet inquiries —I hope—about a few others."

I looked at him anxiously. "Colonel Primrose," I said.

He smiled wryly. "Yes, Mrs. Latham."

"What about Steve—and that gun?"

He shook his head. "I can't tell you about Steve. The gun was there yesterday morning. I felt it under a pile of papers when I was leaning on the edge of the table, when we were talking about the telegrams. The girl at the desk gave me her version of that little incident, by the way. I hope it teaches you a lesson—though I haven't any confidence it will. Anyway, the gun was there. I didn't know it wasn't sealed."

"How many people knew it was there—and not sealed?" I asked.

"I've wondered about that. Mrs. Chapman certainly made no effort to hide it. Moreover, the sitting room door wasn't locked at any time that I know of. I went there twice myself yesterday—once hunting you, once to speak to Mrs. Chapman. No one was in either time. The doors into the adjoining bedrooms were locked, but I assume the sitting room door was left open because you were all using it, and coming and going. There's no reason why anyone who wished to shouldn't have gone in and taken the gun."

"But it wasn't loaded," I said. "Mrs. Chapman unloaded it."

"And put the shells in her pocket?" he inquired with a smile.

"I don't recall," I retorted. "She didn't throw them in the fire, anyway."

"It doesn't matter. George had a case of them on his dresser. There are six missing out of it.—However, that's not what interests me the most. What I want to know is how

George happened to be at that particular spot at that particular time. I'd like to know whether it just happened, or was pre-arranged. Because it happens that a number of people who're involved happened to be there around that time last night."

"Who?"

"Your friends Mrs. Chapman and Joe Anders, for example. And Steve Grant. We saw Mrs. Chapman pick up Steve—presumably—in there somewhere. He was headed that way earlier and he was in the car with her a few minutes later. They were going to Squaw Lake to get Anders.—Who, by the way, made a three-day trip in two days. And the horses look it. I was out there this morning."

"But surely . . ." I began.

"Will you quit saying 'But surely . . .' to me, my dear?" he said patiently. "If you're going to be devil's advocate, get one client and stick to him. Don't defend everybody; I don't know whether you realize it, but the only person you've really defended—and very effectively, I may say—is the one person you'd like to hang. It just happens that Fate, not the law, has circumvented Mr. Ridley and saved his daughter. Everything you told me last night, which you thought was damning Ridley, was helping him, in fact."

"All right," I said. "Go on. Joe didn't like George. But if he'd wanted to kill him, he could have done it easier on the other side of the lake. But do go on."

"I didn't say that," he replied. "The fact is, however, I've never been associated with a case before in which nobody involved either has or pretends to have an alibi of any kind. Even Ridley can't seriously believe his wife's being asleep in a dark trailer constitutes a very good one."

He put down his coffee cup and looked at me with a smile.

"I envy you your sublime capacity for seeing things the way you want them to be. I'd like to be able to think the Chapman crowd are all lily-white, and Lisa and her mother and the two youngsters in the trailer were saved by the hand of God—not by one of their own hands, perhaps."

He looked at his watch.

"I'm meeting the Chief Ranger and Buck. Sorry you can't come along. I'd like to keep you in sight just to keep you out of trouble. But this seems to be pretty much a man's world out here—possibly it's just as well to have one left somewhere."

As we left the dining room Pearl was watching us out of the corner of one mascara-lashed eye. The expression in her face—its softness congealed so that it looked a little the texture of a pink-and-white marzipan pig—said, as clearly as if her flat coastal voice was saying it aloud, "No lousy so-an-so is going to make a fool of me." It seemed to me it was directed as much at what she suspected now was behind the brassy dead pan of Sergeant Buck, the gay deceiver, as what she was convinced was behind my own.

I left the Colonel on the steps under the portico as the Chief Ranger's car turned up the drive, and went back into the lounge. As I turned at the desk to go to my room, I saw Cecily coming rapidly down the corridor. Half way along she raised her head. She glanced behind her, came on quickly and took hold of my arm.

"Come with me—can you?" she said. I looked at her anxious face, a little pale around the full red outline of her lips.

"What *is* the matter?" I demanded.

A sudden irrational sense of foreboding sharpened my voice. She was a completely different Cecily from the dozen or more I'd spent the last two weeks with. She was very young and worried, but chiefly she was horribly frightened. The awareness of it came as a shock to me. She'd been furiously angry, sparklingly gay and wretchedly unhappy, but so far she hadn't been frightened. The fact that there was anything under the face of heaven that could give her eyes the look they had in them now, I should never have believed.

"Let's get away from here, quickly," she said, glancing back down the corridor again. Her fingers tightened on my arm. "Bill stayed out at Squaw Lake to keep the horses while Joe and the cook stock up. They won't need the car till later, so we can take it."

We hurried out the door into the courtyard. I got into the front seat. Cecily didn't, not immediately. She went around looking at each of the tires, got in the back seat, picked up the rugs, shook them out, put them on the seat, raised the leather-covered foot rest, dropped it again, got out and got under the wheel.

"I wish you'd tell me what's the matter," I repeated as we turned down across the wooden bridge. She'd started the other way first, the way George Pelham had gone to his final settlement, and shifted quickly, remembering it.

She didn't bother to answer me. "Where's Colonel Primrose?"

"He just left with the Chief Ranger," I said. "They went this way." I pointed to the right in the direction of West Thumb. She turned the big red car to the left.

"I've got to find Steve," she said. "I've simply got to."

We went along the lake shore past the store. I glanced up at the Winstons' trailer, bright and new and streamlined, among the half dozen grey-and-black homemade jobs scattered through the naked trunks under the high tufted canopy of logpole pines. The gay red-and-white-striped awning was up, but there was no one in the canvas chairs in front of it, and the door was closed. Just as we came into sight of the bleached white antlers over the door of the Ranger Station, a green truck filled with CCC boys in blue dungarees pulled up. Cecily's foot pressed on the gas. We came up beside it as two rangers in the cab with the driver piled out with their gear. One of them stopped.

For a moment I didn't recognize Steve Grant. He was covered with dust. His face was black, his shirt torn and his boots caked with ash and cinders. The back of one of his hands was bleeding through the blue bandanna wrapped around it. He motioned the truck to go on, and came across to us, his eyes fixed on the girl beside me at the wheel.

My heart sank. Something more than a forest fire had happened to Steve. I saw Cecily's eyes meet his. For an instant— and if he hadn't been blind just then he could have seen it— there was so much in them that I looked away quickly. Then when I heard her voice I knew all of it was gone again, and that what was in them now would match the challenge and anger in his own.

"Steve—I'm sorry about last night," she said quickly. "I came to tell you this morning and you were gone."

He didn't answer. He just stood there, looking as if what he'd like to do more than anything else, just then, would be to break her stubborn little neck.

"—I've got to see you, Steve. I'm sorry! I know you despise me, but you've got to help me. It's about grandmother."

He wiped the grimy perspiration out of his eyes with his torn sleeve.

"It's too bad you didn't think of that last night," he said calmly. But it was only his voice that was calm, and that took an effort. "What's happened?"

"Can you come . . . somewhere?"

He nodded and picked up his axe. "Wait till I get a little of this off." As he strode through the door of the Station I looked at Cecily. She'd slumped down on the small of her back behind the wheel, both hands gripping it, staring straight ahead of her.

"Wouldn't you rather I called on the Winstons?" I asked.

111

"No," she said quickly. She was more like her grandmother —and herself—than she'd been before, but the delicate skin around her lips was still white—whiter now that two hot flushed patches burned in her cheeks.

Steve Grant came out, a little cleaner and with a whole shirt. He got in the back of the car and pushed the rugs on the floor. Cecily ran us up the road about a hundred yards and pulled off to the side. She turned, facing Steve over the red leather back of the seat.

"I wouldn't bother you if there was anybody else," she said. I could hear the old struggle in her voice between pride and desperation. But Steve was deaf and stupid as well as blind and stupid. I could have shaken him, except that I was too worried just then to care very much, except that he was making it harder for her to say what she wanted to say than it should have been.

"—Steve! Grandmother didn't . . . she *didn't* do it, did she?"

He looked at her steadily for a moment.

"Of course she didn't. Who says she did?"

"Nobody, yet," Cecily said. "But they were there this morning badgering her again about the gun, asking all sorts of questions. Where she was, why she didn't like George, what she did with the shells she took out of the gun. They left, and then they came back again and asked the same things over again."

Steve was leaning forward, his face pretty grim. "What did she say?"

"Oh, you know how she is. She said it was none of their business why she didn't like George. It was a fact, and they could take it or leave it. She'd told them all she knew about the gun, and they could draw any conclusions they liked. She'd come back from picking up Joe at Squaw Lake, and she was in her room from ten o'clock on."

Steve nodded. "Well?" he asked curtly.

"Well, that's it," Cecily said. "She wasn't. I went in to see her at quarter past ten, and she wasn't there. And that's not the worst of it. Just a few minutes ago I went in your room, Grace—I thought you were in there. It must have been the maid. I heard Mr. Ridley talking next door. He was saying, 'It doesn't matter—Mrs. Chapman wasn't in her room.' I know it wasn't proper to listen, but I did just the same."

Since I had myself been listening like a cat at a mousehole for some days, that impropriety left me unmoved.

"—I wanted to find out what else he'd say. He said, 'And

112

moreover, my dear, she bribed the watchman to leave the door at the end of the hall open. I heard her doing it. I don't want to seem openly to be directing attention toward her . . . but if you could say you *thought* you heard her . . . Anyone can hear her a mile off.' Mrs. Ridley said, 'But I didn't,' and he cut her off. 'I said you could say you *thought* you heard her, my dear. You can be mistaken, you know, but it will start them on her track anyway. They'll find out about the door—and that will be sufficient.' "

I looked around at Steve. If, as my son had said, he was going to smear George, he looked just then as if he could smear Alexander Ridley completely out of existence. His cigarette had burned to a long grey cylinder of ash.

Cecily's voice was frightened and urgent. "Where was she, Steve? Oh, don't you see! She *could* have done it! It's horrible to say, but it's true, and it's all my fault. She knew I was just . . . just making a mess of things. She'd tried every other way to stop it. Then after you . . . came back, and she thought George had—oh well, you know—she was ready to do anything. She loves you more than she does me, or . . . or any of us."

His eyes were fixed out somewhere beyond the middle of the blue shimmering lake. He didn't speak for a moment.

"—I don't know where she was," he said then. "She phoned me the pack was coming in, and she was going over to pick up Joe, and would I meet her up there on the road. We got Joe. They dropped me behind the station."

"Did she say anything?"

"She said plenty," he answered grimly. "I don't know how much of it she meant."

He stopped, and when he went on his voice was very grave. "A lot of it, I guess."

"Isn't there *anything* we can do?" Cecily whispered. "We've got to do something!"

It should have been warm, sitting there in the open car in the blazing sun, but I was cold. My hand against my cheek was like a piece of ice. I didn't look at either of them. There was something too awful about the definite, if not calm, assumption that the square-jawed frosty-eyed old lady could have shot down a man in cold blood without turning a hair. The fact that in my heart I knew the assumption—at least— was perfectly correct didn't make it any less bizarre or astonishing. My mind flew back across the lake to that evening at Mariposa. "There's nothing I wouldn't do to stop it, Grace— nothing." That was before Steve appeared. She'd have said it a hundred times more grimly after that had happened, I knew.

"Joe would have helped her," Cecily said, with simply devastating matter-of-factness. "He'd do anything she told him to."

"He might very easily have done it himself, without any outside suggestion," I was surprised to hear myself say. They didn't seem to be surprised at all. Cecily's brow clouded. "Joe killed a cattle thief two years ago," she said calmly. "He's awfully apt to shoot first and ask questions later.—But that isn't what happened to George. Oh, it's horrible!"

She whispered the words passionately, interrupting herself.

"I don't feel any of the things I should. I don't seem to care really that poor George is . . . is dead. It just doesn't seem——"

She stopped abruptly. Steve looked at her, sitting there behind the enormous old wheel, her small bright head high, her eyes wide, her lips pressed together to keep them from trembling. I saw the old expression—the one before his angry resentment at her for lashing out not at him but at her grandmother the night before—come back into his eyes. The ache in them had softened to something more complex than just the hungry longing he'd watched her with before.

"She won't be hurt by it, Cecily," he said quietly. "I'll see to that. Will you leave it to me? You know I . . . I think she's pretty swell, don't you?"

"Oh yes!" Cecily whispered quickly.

"Then leave it to Uncle Steve, will you, freckle-face?"

She batted her eyes to keep back the sharp tears, and nodded, not turning around.

"Okay, then," he said, with an airy nonchalance that he must have been far from feeling. "Let's get back. Maybe I can do a little work on Mr. Alexander Ridley before I change. I wouldn't want to get my other clothes dirty."

She flashed around then. "Oh no, Steve! Please—you mustn't!"

"Will you drive back to the Ranger Station, please, Miss Chapman?" he said calmly. "You're interfering with government employees in the efficient functioning of their duties, punishable by fine or imprisonment or both."

"But Steve——"

"Are you going to drive this hook-and-ladder back to the Station, sugar, or am I going to dump you out up there, and do it myself?"

She turned on the ignition and started the car. "All I mean is——"

"All I mean is," Steve said, "you keep your snub little nose out of this. Remember the cow poke at Cinnabar that used to say, 'I declare, Cecily's goin' to be as perty as a spotted pup, some a these days, but right now for cri'sake she ain't got the sense of a goose headin' south.' Now step on it, spotted pup, and look out for that truck."

She swerved the car to avoid instant demolition, and laughed infectiously. It was a sudden warm dusky-velvet sound that broke through days of gloom and conflict like the sun out of a three weeks' thunder storm. I hadn't heard it since we'd left Southeast Arm coming from Thorofare, and it was like water springing up in a desert as far as I was concerned. But most such water is mirage, so I suppose I should have realized that this was too—only just then I had no way of telling how far Steve Grant was prepared to go, or what it was he'd so blithely undertaken.

15

Cecily pulled the car up in front of the Ranger Station. Steve got out and stood there a moment with his foot on the running board, looking at her with a smile in his eyes. She held out her hand.

"Be careful, Steve—please?" she said unsteadily.

He took her hand, gave it a tight squeeze. "Okay," he said. He went on quickly into the Station.

The smile faded slowly from her face as she started the car again. "I hope he's not going to . . . do anything crazy," she said slowly.

"He won't," I said.

"I don't know. People do crazy things. And—well, when Steve does one, it's crazier than anybody else would ever think of. He . . . he hasn't changed very much."

There was a touch of wistfulness about her that was rather unexpected. "The wranglers used to say he ate locoweed instead of spinach."

She laughed again.

"We used to have a lot of fun."

She shook her head, and added with sardonic brightness, "Fadeout of Miss Chapman regretting her lost youth."

"Followed," I remarked pleasantly, "by close-up of Miss

Chapman nearly hitting another truck." I grabbed the door as we swerved out again, practically landing in the lake. "If Miss Chapman will watch the road instead of the Ranger Station, she may still be here to enjoy her future. Anyway, think of my motherless children."

She laughed. "If the other one's like Bill, they'll manage very nicely."

And then, as I looked at her, I saw the skin around her lips go deadly white. She caught her breath sharply. I looked quickly up at the hotel. The Chief Ranger's car was standing in the drive under the massive white yellow portico. He and Colonel Primrose were getting out of the front seat. What was alarming was that Joe Anders was getting out of the back, just behind him the massive granite figure of Sergeant Phineas T. Buck. There was nothing at any time that might be called malleable about a posterior view of Sergeant Buck, but when he had a malefactor in tow he had a kind of ramrod inflexibility that I'd seen before and recognized now with a dull feeling in the pit of my stomach.

Cecily put her foot down on the accelerator. We sped through the fifteen-mile zone at fifty, went around the corner into the road across the narrow wooden bridge—fortunately unoccupied at the moment—and came to a sharp stop in the back of the hotel. We got out and went rapidly across the dusty court yard and into the lounge. My friend Pearl, still in her bright pink slacks, was standing by a tub of oleanders, craning her neck at what I assumed was the vanishing figure of her gentleman friend. Before we had time to cross in front of the telephone and transportation desk to see for ourselves, my other friend the bellboy dashed up.

"Mrs. Chapman's certainly receiving a delegation of brass hats," he announced happily.

I felt rather than saw Cecily sway a little and catch herself against the edge of the telephone desk. Her face was frozen the color of parchment. She smiled brightly at the bellboy.

"Do you want to wait a minute, Grace? I've got to phone."

I nodded. She slipped through the tiny office and into the booth. The operator said, "Lake Government," and plugged in and out in the mysterious ritual of the switchboard.

The bellboy said, "It certainly is a lovely day."

"It certainly is," I said.

"Going to be with us a while, I hope?"

"Oh, I'll be here until the winter snows, I'm afraid," I said. He nodded at Pearl, who'd wandered away from the oleander tub, still keeping an eye on me. "She's talking about leaving."

"Really?"

"She was before lunch. It looks like maybe she's changed her mind."

It did indeed. She'd settled down in a strategically advantageous position in the middle of the lounge, opened a movie magazine and a large pink box of chocolates, looking very much as if she'd hibernated. She sat there a long time, turned the magazine right side up, and was still sitting there when Cecily came out of the phone booth.

"Let's hurry," she whispered.

We did—down the corridor past the elevator and up the stairs to our level . . . neither of us speaking, both of us pretty worried, Cecily I knew desperately so.

At her grandmother's sitting room door we stopped. I could hear a man's voice through the door. For a moment I didn't quite recognize that it was Colonel Primrose speaking. His voice was more like the traditional machine gun rattle of the Army than I'd heard it.

"—These are the facts, Mrs. Chapman. Explain them, please."

Cecily opened the door with a quick decisive turn of her hand. She halted an instant inside the room, then went quickly over to her grandmother on the wicker sofa and sat down beside her. I closed the door. Colonel Primrose glanced at me as if he'd never had the pleasure of meeting me, and didn't want it now. He turned back to Mrs. Chapman, sitting there calm and collected as a Buddha, a grim little smile on her lips. her eyes pale-blue and frost-bitten, not amused and not afraid. For an instant, with her granddaughter there beside her, they looked grotesquely like a small elegant terrier protecting a large English bulldog, except that Cecily was more like a slim bright flame.

"Sit down, all of you," Mrs. Chapman said, mildly for her. "And don't try to bully me, Colonel Primrose. When there's bullying to be done, I'm accustomed to doing it myself."

I looked about the room. Sergeant Buck was in his customary place by the door. He looked more like the petrified tree I'd seen on my tour with my old school friend than the tree looked itself. Joe Anders lowered his long lean frame, still in blue jeans but clean ones, his orange silk kerchief still around his neck, into the chair next to the Chief Ranger's. His face was as congealed as Sergeant Buck's, expressionless except for a wary watchfulness in his black eyes.

"I'm not bullying you, Mrs. Chapman," Colonel Primrose said patiently. The rap-rap-rap had left his voice, but it seemed to me the calm impertubability of it was more dangerous.

"I'm merely pointing out to you there are a number of things that have to be explained."

He stopped abruptly, listening, just as I saw Cecily's head go up and her eyes change. Rapid steps were coming down the hall. They came nearer and nearer, and stopped outside the door. Sergeant Buck glanced at his Colonel and jerked the door open. Steve Grant stood in the doorway for an instant, his eyes moving about the room. He stepped inside.

"I guess I'm in on this, sir," he said curtly.

"I guess you are too, Grant," Colonel Primrose replied. "Come in."

He nodded at the chair next to him.

"And now I don't want to be interrupted again. These are facts. Sergeant Buck has gathered them and substantiated them. So far we've made no effort to interpret them. I'm not sure they don't interpret themselves.—Pelham was trying to marry your granddaughter, Mrs. Chapman, and you were opposed to it."

"Bitterly, and unalterably," said Mrs. Chapman.

"You had Pelham's gun in your possession. If you gave it to Grant to have it sealed the night before, as Miss Cecily says you did, he didn't take it. It was here yesterday morning."

Mrs. Chapman's jaw hardened. She said nothing.

"You left the hotel a little before half-past nine last night. You picked up Steve Grant in the road behind the trailer camp. You went to Squaw Lake, picked up Anders, and returned to the hotel a few minutes after ten o'clock."

"After dropping Steve at the Ranger Station," Mrs. Chapman put in brusquely.

Colonel Primrose shook his head. "No," he said. "Not at the Ranger Station. In the road again, approximately where you picked him up. You then came back here. You told us that you and Mr. Anders were here from then until we saw you later. That, Mrs. Chapman, is not true."

"Very well," Mrs. Chapman said. "Go on."

"Yesterday evening at about eight o'clock—after your granddaughter returned from her proposed trip to Gardiner, having been stopped at the Park gate—you spoke to the night watchman. You asked him to leave the door at the end of the hall open until eleven o'clock. He agreed to do it. Before you left, you asked George Pelham to meet you at the Lodge some time after ten-thirty, and you told him the shortest way was along the back road behind the trailer camp. You and Anders left the hotel. Anders went around and picked up your car. You met him at the corner of the building and got in. We don't know when you returned. We do know that George Pelham was alive when you left at a quarter past ten, and that he was dead when you returned. And that the gun——"

The chair next to mine grated across the floor. Colonel Primrose looked around. Steve Grant had got to his feet and was standing there, composed and at ease.

"All that is perfectly true, Colonel Primrose," he said calmly. "Mrs. Chapman and Anders and I were going to pick Pelham up and take him for a ride in the country, just to get him to see some reason. Mrs. Chapman wasn't going to shoot him. Neither was Anders or I. We didn't have the gun. Pelham had it himself. I saw him take it yesterday morning, when he reached over to that table for an ashtray. He put the gun in his pocket. He still had it when I met him in the road before Mrs. Chapman and Anders got there. He started to ride me about being a cripple, and about John Brice and the forged check. I got sore and started to let him have one. He pulled the gun on me. I grabbed his wrist, and the gun went off in his face. He went down, I ducked through the trees behind the trailers. Mrs. Chapman and Joe came up a minute later. They saw him, and I went out and told them what had happened.

"And now I'm telling you. I killed George in self-defence . . . just as I killed Brice. Only there's one thing I didn't do: I never forged a check."

The room was so silent I could hear the gulls screaming far out on the lake.

Colonel Primrose's sparkling black X-ray eyes rested steadily on Steve Grant's face. Then he nodded his head.

"Thanks, Grant," he said quietly. "That's pretty much what I thought. I just wanted to be sure."

Cecily was staring at him, her face as white and cold as marble. Suddenly she sprang to her feet.

"*Steve!*" she cried. "It's not true! Colonel Primrose, don't believe him! It's a lie! Oh, grandmother, don't let them take him! It's a lie, you know it is!"

Mrs. Chapman sat slumped down at the end of the sofa,

her face limp, her lips very blue. She closed her eyes. I stared at her in horror. It wasn't a lie. I could tell by the way her head moved forward that it wasn't a lie at all. It was the truth.

16

I sat there stunned. I'd listened to Steve's calm matter-of-fact recital with astonishment, I'll admit, but with the complacent conviction at the same time that it wasn't true, and that there wasn't any use being disturbed, because it wouldn't fool anybody. It wouldn't be the first time a young man had stepped forward with his head bared to the executioner's stroke to save somebody he loved. Until I'd seen Mrs. Chapman after Cecily's appeal, I'd thought it was precisely what one would have expected him to do. I'd been perfectly confident, up to then, that as soon as Steve finished, Colonel Primrose would smile, the way he does, and say, as I'd heard him say on at least two similar occasions, "That's all very nice, Grant, but . . ." and then calmly and politely show it didn't make sense in the least—that at the moment of the murder the young man was well known to have been holding a skein of knitting yarn for his deaf and aged aunt, or something.

So I was completely unprepared for what he did say, and even more unprepared for Mrs. Chapman's shattering acceptance of a statement that I now saw she'd known was true but had hoped desperately would never be made . . . and that she'd have denied with all her soul, at any cost, if she could have done it with the least hope of success. And if I was stunned—and I was—it was nothing to what Cecily was like. She just sat there like a small flame-tipped pillar of salt, her face bloodless, all life drained out of her.

Colonel Primrose looked from Mrs. Chapman to Joe Anders, and back again. Mrs. Chapman made a tragic effort to get control of herself again. She moistened her blue lips and gripped the arm of the sofa with one square capable hand until her white knuckles stood out like marbles.

"It's my fault, Colonel Primrose, entirely," she said. "I told Steve I was going to get Joe to help me scare the liver out of George. It was so white I knew it wouldn't take much to do it. I wanted to put off the marriage he and his brother-in-law were stampeding my granddaughter into when she was in no state to think—only to act, and that very unwisely in my opinion."

She folded her hands in her lap. In spite of all her efforts, all the fight had gone out of her grim square old face. She sat there, nothing but a desperately unhappy old woman who'd staked everything on one last throw and lost.

"I told Steve not to come—it wasn't his party, it was mine and Joe's," she said heavily. I didn't know George had the gun, though I should have, I suppose. I didn't even know it was gone. I hadn't thought about it since the night before. I was almost out of my mind all day. When Cecily came back, not married, I made up my mind to put a stop to another such expedition, if I could, as the only effective thing I could think of, until we were back East again and Cecily had time to think and listen to reason. It may have been rough justice, but people like George aren't open to any other kind. I'm sorry—not because of what happened to George, because I think he's been asking for it, but because of Steve. George wasn't fit to wipe the dust off his boots."

There was a long silence. Colonel Primrose was still looking from one to another of them. He held out his hand to the Chief Ranger. "May I have that telegram?"

He took the yellow envelope that Mr. Rayburn handed him and opened it, turning to Steve.

"It seems to me, Grant," he said soberly, "that it's time we had your version of that check. It wasn't forged, by the way. It was raised."

He held out the telegram.

"This is from Chapman and Davis. It will probably interest all of you. It says:

"This office has no memorandum in re Stuyvesant check incident. Investigation handled privately and confidentially through George Pelham who reported personally to Mr. Chapman. Mr. Pelham has only first-hand information obtained. Suggest you contact him care Chapman, Cinnabar Ranch, Elk Hole, Wyoming."

His eyes rested steadily on Steve's.

"I don't think there's anybody here," he went on, "who doubts that Pelham was capable of distorting information to his own ends, Grant. You were presumably dead, in this case. There was nothing you could do about it. Suppose you tell us what happened."

Steve hesitated just an instant. "I'm perfectly willing to tell you what happened," he said evenly. "You can take it or leave it. This fellow Brice was our mail clerk. A friend of mine in another house dropped in the office one day and saw him, and about dropped dead. Brice had been in his place three weeks before and opened an account for himself, giving us as a reference, and handed over his check for ten thousand dollars, with an order to buy Associated Steel at twenty-four. He called up every morning about eleven and gave his order for the day, and at the end of a couple of weeks he'd made something over six thousand. One morning he went in and collected his nine thousand five hundred and started playing with the six thousand.

"It looked like hanky-panky to me, so I started tracking it down. I found out the day he'd opened the account we'd got a letter from a crazy old girl I did business for, enclosing a check for ten dollars for a basket of fruit to send to a boat, to a clergyman who was going to Europe. I found out she hadn't sent a check but a ten dollar bill. The cashier hadn't thought anything about it. She did crazy things. He figured she'd written the letter and changed her mind and put the cash in instead.

"I went around to see her. Her bank statement had just come in. Her checks always looked more like scratchings than writing anyway, and she never paid any attention to her account, either with us or the bank, as long as she didn't lose any money. I went over her statement, and I found the check for ten thousand written on the 2nd of the month, and a cash deposit of ten thousand two weeks later. All she knew was she hadn't written a check for ten thousand, though she frequently did, and she hadn't deposited ten thousand that month. Well, I went around and got Brice and dragged him in by the scruff of the neck. He went all to pieces and admitted the whole thing. He pulled in a heartrending story about his old father in a home for incurables—he didn't say it was a charity home and he'd never been near it since the old man was admitted.

"Anyway, Mrs. Stuyvesant was a great old gal. She said it was wonderful and we ought to let Brice run the shop—he seemed to know more about the market than we did. Just the same, she didn't want to deal with a firm that had a wizard for a mail clerk. If he got out, she wouldn't do anything about it, and she'd let him keep the wad he'd made to make his old man's last days happy."

He grinned sardonically.

"He quit, all right, telling the office boy I was hounding him out of the office. Two weeks later I found he'd got a job in the bank that had Mrs. Stuyvesant's account. I didn't want to hound him out of that, so I got her a machine to write her checks with. She used it about a week and went back to her scratching, so I told her Brice was in the bank. She got the wind up and had him fired. He started buying on margin and went out, and then he started following me around, getting seedier and seedier. He didn't shave and he got a wild look in his eyes. Then the night——"

He hesitated, not looking at Cecily.

"——The night I left the Chapmans, he was crouching down behind the seat. I didn't see him till we'd got out in the road. He climbed over the seat and stuck a gun in my ribs. He was cockeyed. I thought he was doped, he was so wild. He said I was persecuting him, and a lot of stuff. I tried to tell him he was crazy, until he said he was going to kill me anyway.

"Well, I didn't give a damn whether he killed me or not, to tell the truth, but I figured it might as well be both of us and not just me. So I stepped on it and went into the next telephone pole. When I came to I was in the bottom of a ditch. It was almost daylight. The car was dumped over and burned to cinders. There was a milk truck had just stopped. I heard a fellow say, 'Even his old ma won't recognize that baby.' I tried to get up and call, but they didn't hear me. What they'd said kept going through my mind, and I . . . well, if it had been me it would have saved a lot of trouble."

He still didn't look at Cecily, but he was talking to her now, not anybody else.

"My pal George hadn't wanted to hurt my feelings. He'd been as decent about it as he could, and of course Cecily couldn't come right out and say she didn't want to marry a cripple and that I'd changed while I was away. But I . . . I must have noticed she was upset when I was down, and of course she'd go through with it, because that was the kind of girl she was. But I'd noticed she didn't write as often——"

Cecily, who'd been listening to him, lips parted, amber-flecked eyes wide, sprang suddenly to life.

"Steve—that's not true! George mailed my letters in town because they went quicker by air, and it took days from the country! It was you that didn't write to me!"

He looked at her silently for a moment. "I sent my letters by George too," he said, with sardonic bitterness. "That was his idea. Your father's runner was taking them down at night."

Cecily closed her eyes, the tears squeezing under her gold-tipped lashes.

"My pal George said you wanted to marry him, but you felt too sorry for me. I . . . well, I didn't want you to feel sorry for me. So I . . . pulled out. The way a fellow I saw in a movie about a train wreck did. I . . . well, you see, freckle-face, I loved you so much I could take anything but your . . . sacrificing yourself. So, I——"

Well, I don't suppose three years is a terribly wide chasm to jump, not when it's contracted into the narrow space of a hotel room. I don't know which of them jumped it first, but I know they met practically in the center of the room in each other's arms. I also know I shouldn't have had the grace not to simply sit and stare at them if I hadn't seen Sergeant Buck forget he was house-broken and spit neatly on the floor before he averted his eyes and cleared his iron-bound throat with a loud clatter that sounded like a freight train with a flat wheel crossing a trestle.

I looked at Colonel Primrose. He was looking at the floor, scratching his head and smiling a little, and Mrs. Chapman was sitting there on the sofa, tears pouring down her cheeks that hadn't, I suspect, ever felt salt water, except in the ocean, for seventy-five years.

Colonel Primrose cleared his own throat then.

"Well, before we can hang you, Grant," he said politely, "I'm afraid you're going to have to clear up one or two little points."

Cecily flashed around, her eyes wild in an instant.

"How long, for instance, did you and Pelham talk, before he pulled out his gun?"

Steve stood there silently for a moment. "About . . . five minutes, I guess. No longer than that."

Colonel Primrose nodded very affably.

"The District Ranger," he went on slowly, "says you didn't leave his quarters until almost twenty minutes past ten. You were listening to a news commentator who came on at ten. The program changed at ten-fifteen. You got up, got your hat, got a drink of water and talked to him a minute or so from the kitchen before you went out. He'd just walked back into the living room and sat down when he heard the shot. You couldn't possibly have got as far as the Winstons' trailer, even if you'd run like hell."

There was another instant of silence in the room. Mrs. Chapman rose abruptly to her feet.

"Steve!" she said. "For the love of God! You . . . you didn't think *I* killed . . . Oh, Steve, you precious imbecile!"

Cecily turned back to him, her eyes like stars.

"Steve—were you . . . were you lying about everything . . . I mean, about you and George—out there?"

He looked down at her upturned face as if nothing had ever mattered, really, or ever would again. "Sure," he said. I don't think it made much difference to him, just then, whether they hanged him or anybody else.

"Well," Colonel Primrose said patiently, "some of us are rather busy. I'd like to know what really did happen, now that you three—I take it—don't think each of the others is a murderer. Mrs. Chapman, you are still sane, I hope?"

"I hope so, Colonel Primrose," she said tartly. "I haven't any confidence about it."

It was wonderful to hear the old war horse paw the ground again. And to see Sergeant Buck congeal into granite again, and slip one foot aside to obliterate his lapse from customary domestic usage.

"We heard a shot," Mrs. Chapman went on. "I was scared, frankly. I started the car, and choked it. I got it going finally. It couldn't have been very long, actually. When I got there, Joe was kneeling down beside George."

She looked at Joe Anders, who nodded silently.

"He didn't say anything. He just picked up the gun and handed it to me. Just then Steve came up, from behind the trailers. I said, 'What shall we do?' We just stood there for a minute. Joe said, 'That's the gun Pelham said you took the seals off for him at Cabin Creek, Steve.' Steve said, 'Like hell I did.' Joe took it and wiped it off with his handkerchief and dropped it on the ground. I told them we'd better get out— let you figure it out the best you could. Steve said he'd have to report it, and I said he'd do nothing of the sort. I didn't think he'd done it, but I thought it might be pretty hard for any of us to explain, and somebody would be bound to find him any minute, with all the savages twosing it about in the dark. It seemed to me least said, soonest mended."

"Not, frankly, caring very much," Colonel Primrose observed dryly, "who'd done it now it was done."

"You took the words out of my mouth, Colonel."

He turned to Steve.

"You passed the Winstons' trailer. Did you see anyone leave it, or come back to it?"

I thought, "Oh, *dear*." We were back to that poor woman.

Steve frowned. "No, I don't recall anything," he said slowly. "I was going as fast as I could, after I heard the shot.

I wasn't thinking about the trailer. Anyway, when I got there and saw Mrs. Chapman standing over George with a gun in her hand, I didn't think about anything else."

"It would have been simple enough for anyone to dodge around the trailer closest to the road and slip back to the Winstons', without your seeing him?"

Steve nodded.

"In fact, someone could have been behind it while the three of you were standing there?"

Steve nodded again. "Yes."

"It's an interesting point," Colonel Primrose remarked. "I think we might follow it up, Buck, if you're not being busy this evening."

Sergeant Buck's lantern-jawed dead pan suffused itself with dull rose, so that he looked like a slab of Yellowstone's volcanic rhyolite. Nevertheless he came smartly to attention, saluting not in fact but in effect. "Yes, sir," he said out of one corner of his mouth. "I mean, no, sir."

He opened the door. The Chief Ranger held his hand out to Steve with a smile. "Expect you back on the job tomorrow, Grant," he drawled. Colonel Primrose stopped a moment as he passed me.

"Will you be very careful and not do anything impulsive for a couple of hours, Mrs. Latham?" he said in a low undertone. His face was so sober in contrast to the Chief Ranger's broadly smiling countenance that I was taken aback.

"I mean it seriously, my dear."

I nodded. It was almost five o'clock, and there wasn't much I could do, impulsive or otherwise, before dinner. Nevertheless the perturbation in his eyes was sufficiently disturbing to make me feel a little like the skeleton at the feast after Buck closed the door behind them.

Mrs. Chapman got up. "I'll take you back, Joe, and pick up Bill. Do you want to come, Grace? I expect Cecily and Steve have a few things to catch up on."

For a moment I started to say yes, and then I didn't. There couldn't be anything particularly impulsive about going to Squaw Lake after my son, but for some curious reason I hesitated. If I stayed in the hotel, I thought, for once Colonel Primrose couldn't accuse me of disobeying orders.

They went out, and I went through Cecily's room toward my own. The maid had left our connecting door open. As I closed it, I heard Colonel Primrose's voice coming from the Ridleys' room. For a moment I hesitated, thinking I ought to go back, and then I changed my mind, thinking that after all

he wouldn't mind my listening in on the next step in his case
So I stayed quietly where I was.

". . . sympathize with Mrs. Ridley's grief," he was saying
"But we feel she'll be as anxious as we are to find out who
killed her brother. If you feel at any point, Mrs. Ridley, that
we're putting you to too great a strain, all you have to do is
say so."

17

I had a clear picture of that room, just then, in my mind's
eye. Colonel Primrose and the Chief Ranger would be standing just inside the door between the open suitcases on the
floor, with Mr. Ridley's large tailored figure sort of blocking
their further entrance as much as he could, trying to ease
them out into the hall. Mrs. Ridley I wasn't quite so sure
about. She couldn't be lying down still, or they wouldn't have
got that far. She was probably sitting over by the window,
shadowy and dowdy in one of her undistinguished print
dresses, completely unnerved without having to pretend to
be.

Mr. Ridley said "Very well," a little shortly, and I could
hear him move aside. "My wife's anxious to help you. She's
not very strong, and this has been a severe shock.—You'll
remember too, I hope, that I'm in the position of her counsel
here, as well as husband."

I could see Colonel Primrose nodding suavely.

"Will you just tell us, quite simply and quietly, Mrs. Ridley,
exactly what you did, last night?"

"But I have already told you that, in some detail—" Mr.
Ridley began.

"—If you please, Mrs. Ridley," Colonel Primrose said. I
listened avidly, a little chill running up and down my spine—
for his tone was not usually as dangerously affable as it was
now.

Mrs. Ridley spoke before her husband could. "Oh, yes,"
she said promptly. "I'm quite fit, Alexander. My headache is
gone. I'd like——"

"Then do, my dear. But don't over-do."

"I went to the Lodge," she said hurriedly. "To see the
young people dance. My husband stayed here. I watched
them a while, and then my head started to ache. I think the
altitude affects me here. The children suggested I go down

to the trailer and take some asperin and lie down until the dance was over. I did, after a while. It was dark, and very quiet. I must have dropped off to sleep, because they woke me up at eleven, when they came in. They persuaded Lisa to spend the night with them. She'd never slept all night in a trailer and we thought it would be fun. So I started back alone. I had on my sapphire and diamond clip. The spring has been weak for some time, and I felt it go loose. I was looking around on the ground for it when I stumbled across . . . my brother."

She spoke hurriedly and monotonously, the way a child does who's learned his piece for the Sunday School entertainment and has the grim figure of his mother sitting in the front row. There was a short silence.

I heard Colonel Primrose. "Is this the clip you lost?"

"Oh, yes!" Mrs. Ridley cried. "I'm so glad you found it!"

"We'll have to keep it a few days, Mrs. Ridley.—You didn't hear the shot, I take it?"

"No. I was asleep."

"You mean you presume you were, my dear," her husband said. "You don't know when the shot was fired, of course."

"That's what I meant," Mrs. Ridley said hurriedly. "I didn't hear it, so I thought I must have been asleep."

"I see," Colonel Primrose said. "And the young people? When they came in they hadn't heard anything?"

"No. They hadn't. I mean, they didn't mention anything, so they couldn't have."

"And they didn't mention anything?"

"No!" Her voice rose a little breathlessly.

"Take it easy, my dear," Mr. Ridley said. "There's nothing to be alarmed at. Is there, Colonel?"

I hoped there was nothing as alarming as it seemed to me in Colonel Primrose's not answering that. "Are you quite sure, Mrs. Ridley," he asked quietly, "that you didn't leave the trailer?"

"Oh, quite!"

"I want you to think a moment. You didn't hear a shot, and get up, and wait a few moments, pretty frightened, not knowing what to do, and finally get up enough courage to go out in the dark?"

"Oh, no!" Mrs. Ridley gasped. "No!"

"You didn't creep around the end of the Winstons' trailer, see someone in the shadows, and steal back, frightened? And creep back again, when you thought everyone had left— and lose your clip then?"

"No!" Mrs. Ridley cried. "No! I didn't——"

Mr. Ridley spoke almost savagely. It was the first time I'd heard his voice perfectly natural and free from artifice when people were around.

"This has gone far enough, Primrose! You're driving my wife mad with your third degree!"

"All right," Colonel Primrose said. I'd never heard his voice more bland, or richer in what Twain called the calm confidence of a Christian with four aces. "That's all, Mrs. Ridley. Thank you. Good afternoon."

I still stood there after the door had closed and the tread of feet had disappeared down the hall. There was a long silence, broken by the sound of Mrs. Ridley weeping quietly. Suddenly she raised her voice.

"Oh, I'm sorry, Alexander. I didn't mean to go all to pieces like that!"

It was so pitifully a defensive wail that I had an instant picture of the wretched women looking at him in terror as he stood by the door.

"Well, my dear," Alexander Ridley's voice said, pleasantly, "if you ignore the advice of counsel, you have to take the consequences. There's not much I can do about it, I'm afraid."

There was silence again. I could hear him walking slowly across the room toward her.

"—Why, may I ask, didn't you tell me they'd found your clip there? You did know it, didn't you? You deceived nobody, if that's any comfort to you."

He lowered his voice a little. "—And why did you lie to me about leaving the trailer?"

I stood there, gasping, not quite sure I'd heard him. It was terribly confusing. If he was convinced, as he obviously was when he accused her flatly of being a murderess, he must have known she'd left the trailer. She could hardly have shot George Pelham from the inside of it.

"I was afraid!" Mrs. Ridley moaned.

Then there was another long silence, and suddenly the most extraordinary thing happened. I heard a suitcase slither across the rug and bump against the wall, and a chair pushed aside. I was still standing in Cecily's open door. At the end of the short passage between my bath on one side and the Ridleys' closet and mine on the other, I could see the thin strip of daylight under the locked door that separated their room from mine. Only I couldn't see it now. A dark shadow had blotted a large portion of it out. And I knew, without having the faintest idea why, that Mr. Ridley had crossed their room and was standing very close to that door. My breath stopped for an instant.

"Alexander!" Mrs. Ridley said, almost sharply.

"Sssh!" he whispered.

There was something about the sound of that hiss that made my throat suddenly dry and constricted. I took a step forward toward my outside door, perplexed and frightened for no good reason that occurred to me. There was a little tap on the connecting door. I didn't answer . . . not because I didn't intend to, but my throat was as dry as grass and no sound came out of it. He tapped again, quite loudly, and called out, so pleasantly that it sent a chill down my spine, "Oh, Mrs. Latham!"

As I started again to answer, something curling around in the bottom of my mind pricked sharply. I took two more steps forward, as silently as I could, with my eye on the hall door. And I saw something that turned me—still for no known reason perfectly frigid with sudden dread. The inside bolt had been turned on it. I had myself locked that door . . . on the outside. It had been locked on the inside by someone else . . . why, I hadn't the foggiest notion.

I heard Mr. Ridley's voice again, much lower.

"—I want to make perfectly sure that cursed woman isn't snooping in there."

He knocked again, this time quite loudly. "Oh, Mrs. Latham—are you in?"

No body will ever be able to tell me why, at that moment, I took a quick noiseless step toward the closet door, slightly ajar, and drew it open with shaking fingers. Just as I did, I heard the door knob turning on the connecting door between me and Mr. Ridley. I slipped into the closet and pulled the door shut behind me, letting the knob turn slowly and silently and the catch slip home as he opened the door between our rooms and came in.

"—Mrs. Latham?" he said.

I shrank against the wall in the dark, terrified for fear I'd rattle the wire hangers on the rod, hardly daring to breathe. I could hear his footsteps cross my floor toward Cecily's room.

"—Miss Chapman?" he said, not loudly but loud enough to be heard if she was in her own room. Then I heard Cecily's door pulled to and the bolt turned. His steps came back closer and closer to the door behind which I was cowering, as terrified now, I think, as I've been for a long time. I heard another bolt turn. He was unlocking my hall door.

I did hold my breath, then. He'd come to the closet next. His heavy tread on the floor sent little shocks through my feet up my spine. He stopped, not two feet, I suppose, from the closet door, and suddenly moved away. I leaned back against the rough plaster wall, my heart pounding in my throat, as I heard his feet in the passage and the door there closing. I didn't move. My knees were shaking like leaves, sere and brown in the winter wind.

"And now, my dear," I could hear him say, his voice like distilled venom. "*Who* did you see when you came out of the trailer?"

I heard the bed bump against the wall as Mrs. Ridley must have backed against it, trying to get away from that voice and the eyes that I knew matched it.

"Nobody!" she gasped. "I didn't see anybody, I tell you! I didn't!"

"You're lying, May," Mr. Ridley said, very calmly. "You're lying. That's why you dared to keep your daughter away from me last night. Don't try to lie now—it's too late, my dear. It's too late. Did you think you were cleverer than I am?"

He laughed then, so softly that I could barely hear him. And as I stood there in that closet, my icy hands shaking, my throat parched, my breath hardly coming at all, the cold chills racing up and down my spine, I didn't yet understand what this was all about . . . not until I heard Mrs. Ridley speak again, still with that helpless hypnotized voice.

"Oh, don't, Alexander! I didn't see you, I swear to God I didn't! That's not why I left Lisa—it was because I was going to run away! I can't stand this any longer!"

As I heard that my heart stopped beating entirely for a dreadful instant, and then raced as I stood, leaning against the closet walls, my hand shaking uncontrollably, just automatically listening.

"Don't shout," Alexander Ridley said, almost agreeably. "I wouldn't want anyone to hear you. Anyway, our friend Mrs. Latham isn't next door to run hot-footed to tell the Colonel. She's been very convenient, I must say. When you want a case put forward, May, the best person to do it is an unconscious friend at court."

Mrs. Ridley spoke, hesitatingly, still in that terrible helpless tone.

"Then you never wanted George to marry that girl! I couldn't understand the way you changed. I do now. You wanted Lisa to get her money—so you could take it away from her."

Mr. Alexander Ridley laughed again.

"Of course I didn't want your brother to marry. Do you think I wanted to wait twenty-two years longer to collect for all the years I've spent with you?"

"—You can't take Lisa's money. It's hers. My father knew you too well!"

"Lisa is very devoted to you, my dear. I think I could have made it worth her while to pay almost anything for your freedom. I could have managed to persuade her to turn over a large part of it, my dear—if it hadn't been for you."

I reached a trembling and icy hand up in the dark and touched the hard icy metal of the door knob. Then I stopped, simply paralyzed with terror, as he spoke again.

"Perhaps it's better this way, dear. Sit down at the desk. I said sit down. Now pick up your pen and write what I tell you to. If you don't my dear, your daughter will certainly have an accident when she comes into her money in a couple of years. That's better. Don't take so much ink on your pen. Now write, 'Colonel Primrose: I killed my brother——"

"I won't——"

"Oh yes you will, May. And you'll do it quickly. Time is passing."

"Alexander, you're hurting me!" she cried suddenly. "I'll write. I'll write anything. Only promise me . . ."

"I'll let Lisa go anywhere she likes and never see her again, if you wish. Now go ahead. 'I killed him to keep him from ruining my daughter's inheritance. I took the gun out of his room. He told my husband he was going to meet Mrs. Chapman at the Lodge at half-past ten. I waited behind the trailer and shot him. I didn't have time to get back before Mrs. Chapman's man came running, and she and Mr. Grant came right after. I hid behind the trailer till they left. Then I slipped back again and waited until the others came.' Now sign it, my dear. 'May Pelham Ridley.'

"Now to your daughter. 'Dearest Lisa. Forgive me, darling. It was the only way I could save you. Remember me always. Mother.' "

There was a little silence then in the other room, broken by a choking cry of sudden terror from Mrs. Ridley. "Alexander—you're not going to——"

"Don't be absurd, my dear," Mr. Ridley said. "I'm not

going to do anything. It's time for our dinner. You're going to put those two notes in your Bible, on the dresser, and comb your hair and come with me to the dining room."

I don't know how much longer it was that I crouched there, my brain beating a nauseating tattoo in my skull. He was going to kill her too. Whether she was too stupid and browbeaten to realize it, or whether she believed his promise to let Lisa go free and was willing to pay any price for that, I didn't know. I only knew that each moment was bringing her nearer and nearer death, and that something had to be done. But I didn't dare move. I couldn't bring myself to let him know I was there—I who'd been his priceless unconscious witness.

I thought of the first day when I'd let my boot fall and he'd gone on talking, and all the other times he must have been waiting, listening, for me to come in, to go on building up the pretence that he wanted his brother-in-law to marry Cecily, that constituted his best and subtlest defence. I remembered what Cecily had said about hearing the maid in my room. How many times, I wondered mechanically, when he'd wanted to say something he didn't want repeated, had he knocked on the door I'd casually assumed was locked, and then come in and found I wasn't there and he was safe? And I thought then of the time he'd openly accused her of murdering her brother. That had been for me to tell the Colonel too. I realized suddenly how much more his interview with Colonel Primrose that morning would have meant if the Colonel had already known—as Mr. Ridley must have assumed he did—that he was convinced the little woman had done it and was nobly perjuring himself in her defence.

"If you're ready, my dear," I heard him say kindly. "You look worn out. I don't want you fainting in public. Take this —I'll get you a glass of water."

My heart stopped. I put my hand back on the door knob and started to turn it. Then I heard Mrs. Ridley's faded voice.

"I've just taken some aspirin. I'll be all right, Alexander. I won't make a scene."

The door opened and closed, I heard their feet pass along the hall in front of my room and fade in the distance.

18

I got out of that closet faster than I'd ever got out of any place in my life. In the dresser mirror I caught a glimpse of my face. It looked as if it had been dipped in the flour barrel. I ran over to the door that separated me from the Ridleys, turned the lock, came back to the dresser, took my hat off and started to take off my jacket. Then I stopped abruptly. If I changed, he'd know I'd been in my room—and that was the last thing I wanted him to know. My heart turned very chilly again as I slipped my jacket back on, put on my hat again and hurried out into the hall.

It was empty except for a testy old gentleman with walrus mustaches and a face as red as a lobster, with a sweet gentle-faced old lady. "Geysers, geysers, geysers!" he was sputtering as I rushed past. "All you see is geysers—bears and geysers!" I could just hear his wife comforting him as best she could: "But Horace, there aren't any geysers here, just a lovely lake . . ."

It seemed incredibly grotesque to me as I got down to the lounge and looked desperately about for Colonel Primrose. He wasn't there. Neither was Sergeant Buck. Pearl was. She was in a pink lace dress with pink gardenias on the shoulder, planted firmly in front of a tub of pink oleanders, watching both doors. She gave me a look intended to be haughty but that was so grimly determined I knew instantly that my childish efforts to save Sergeant Buck had failed. Suddenly she got up, her face breaking into a wreathed effect of girlish smiles. I glanced around and saw the Sergeant coming in. At the sight of his pink lady his rock-ribbed stony face brightened like Yellowstone's famed Obsidian Cliff with the sun on it.

Then, as he saw me, it congealed again to a New England granite in the sultry glow preceding a storm of sheet lightning. I'd taken a step toward him, but I stopped. Mrs. Ridley could have died a thousand deaths before I'd have taken another. I retreated hastily down the empty lounge toward the dining room. It was fortunately one of those quiet evenings of respite, I saw, between plagues of tourists swarming like happy locusts all over the place. The dining room had only a few pleasant people, not bolting their food to catch a bus or hear a lecture.—And one definitely unpleasant one. Mr. Ridley sat with his wife at a small intimate table for two. He looked expansive and pleased with life. And my heart chilled again as I saw her, in spite of all my resolutions to be cool and composed. She looked like a wet sparrow fascinated by a sleek and playful rattlesnake biding its time.

Half a dozen tables beyond them, along the room with its broad windows looking out through the great white fluted columns to the lake glowing softly in the deepening twilight, I saw Mrs. Chapman and my son, and Steve and Cecily. Cecily's face was as radiant as the morning, and Steve—well, I don't think Steve was aware of anything in the room except it. Bill waved and motioned me to a chair, but I shook my head. In front of me, at a table not ten feet from the Ridleys, were Colonel Primrose and the Chief Ranger. There have been several times in the past when I've been so glad to see him I could almost have wept with relief—together with several when I could have done just the opposite—but I have never been as relieved as I was to see him then . . . and so close to Alexander Ridley, even if that meant nothing to him.

I stopped as he pulled out a chair for me. "—Won't you join us?" he asked.

The Chief Ranger got up too, with a little of Sergeant Buck's own fine cordiality, not knowing, I presume, how thoroughly life with Sergeant Buck had inured me to frost of any degree, and sat down again.

Mr. Ridley glanced around. I saw him register my hat and sport jacket and no doubt generally wind-swept appearance, and smile cordially.

"Good evening, Mrs. Latham. Lovely evening, isn't it?"

"Enchanting," I managed to say. "Good evening, Mrs. Ridley."

She gave me a pathetic sort of nod, and went back to the delectable slice of broiled ham hardly touched on her plate. At that moment Pearl made a dramatic entrance with Sergeant Buck in tow. While it had never occurred to me that Sergeant Buck didn't eat, it was the first time I'd ever seen him in the same dining room with his Colonel. Their difference in rank was a fact of life that Buck preserved with such adamant punctiliousness that Colonel Primrose had long ago given up fighting against it.

I glanced at the Colonel. There was a faint amused flicker in his eyes as he handed me the menu. As I took it I thought suddenly of a means I'd been racking my brain to think of. Under cover of it, I pulled a visiting card out of my bag, scribbled on it, my hand shaking so that it was almost illegible, "He's going to kill her," and slipped it aside to him.

His black eyes rested on it for an instant, and he looked up with an amused smile in them. "I'm afraid not," he said, glancing around at his Sergeant. Then, as his eyes met mine and he saw the expression on my face, his gaze sharpened. He sat there staring at me for a moment; and then he glanced almost imperceptibly toward Alexander Ridley, so instantly on the alert, every nerve taut, that I felt an almost sickening sense of relief as I realized he knew already that Mr. Ridley was his man, and that that was why he was there so close to him.

Still holding the menu resting on the table in front of me, I wrote on the bottom of the card, "She knows it. Watch him," smiling with bright fixed attention at the story the Chief Ranger was telling. Colonel Primrose slipped the card into his pocket, his face expressionless. Our conversation went on, not brilliantly, with me racking my brain for questions about volcanoes and geological formations and God knows what else, to keep the Chief Ranger talking so Colonel Primrose could watch. I don't know what I thought Alexander Ridley could do, there in the soft pleasant light of a public dining room, but with those two notes touchingly reposing in Mrs. Ridley's Bible on her dresser I knew time was a factor, and I know that whatever he did would be quick and daring and neat.

And then, so casually and naturally that it didn't occur to me for an instant that the moment had come, he took a small flat yellow tin of aspirin out of his vest pocket, turned it up in his hand, swallowed a tablet, picked up his water glass and washed it down, with a nod to the waitress standing by the serving table. She filled the glass again. Mr. Ridley, lighting a cigarette, pushed it back from his plate with his free hand until it was almost touching his wife's—so easily that even watching him I barely noticed him do it. He glanced at the door, smiling at the apoplectic walrus-mustached old gentleman coming in, leaned forward and said something to Mrs. Ridley. As she glanced around he picked up her glass quite casually, and leaned back in his chair, blowing a feather of white smoke up toward the ceiling.

My heart stopped nauseatingly. Colonel Primrose hadn't moved. And then, just as I looked around at him, his chair went back in a flash and he was around our table and across the space between it and the Ridley's . . . and turned just in time to see Mrs. Ridley there with her hand on her water glass, raising it to her lips. Alexander Ridley's chair went down with a crash. Colonel Primrose took two quick steps past him and caught Mrs. Ridley's arm. I heard the sound of quick running feet, and Alexander Ridley leaped up, his face very white suddenly, just in time to be caught in the grasp of two powerful arms in the olive-green of a uniformed ranger. It was Steve Grant, and he held a struggling snarling figure with effortless strength.

I heard Colonel Primrose say, "Put it down, carefully, Mrs. Ridley," with so much quiet authority that she did it instantly, automatically. He turned back to the white-faced man across the table, Steve Grant's hands still pinioning his arms at his sides. "It's all up, Mr. Ridley," he said calmly. "Take him away, Grant."

He turned to the Chief Ranger. "This is one time when fingerprints mean something. Send that to the F. B. I. in Denver, and handle it carefully.—I'm sorry, Mrs. Ridley," he added gently.

She was still staring at the glass, paralyzed, her face as grey as cigarette ash.

"It's . . . all right," she whispered. "I . . . I knew he was going to kill me."

And then, as I stared at all of them, pretty paralyzed myself, she added what on the whole seems to me the most incongruous remark I've ever heard. "—I . . . I didn't think he'd do it in public."

She tried to get up, clutched at the edge of the table and reeled forward. Colonel Primrose caught her. "Have Bill run over to the Winstons' trailer and bring Lisa," he said to me, over his shoulder. And then, while he was still looking at me, a little flicker moved suddenly in his sparkling black eyes. "And thanks," he said. It was the first time, I may say, that my efforts in the field of crime had ever got anything but a patient smile.

I glanced across the room then, for some reason. Sergeant Phineas T. Buck was still sitting at the table with his pink Dalilah . . . a monolithic Samson, shorn and bound. He hadn't moved. He couldn't, I suppose. Her hand was holding his forearm firmly onto the table; her face was white as dough. I don't imagine that if Old Faithful had suddenly ceased to operate I would have been so surprised, and appalled. And Sergeant Buck's face wasn't white at all. It was just an old, deep, richly burnished copper. He turned his fish-grey eyes away as they met mine.

Pearl smiled sweetly. She'd won the day, and she knew it perfectly.

19

It was two days later that Colonel Primrose and Bill and I were on the dock, saying goodbye to Mrs. Chapman, on her way back across the Southeast Arm of the lake to Thorofare and Cinnabar.

Steve was helping Cecily into her green oilskin coat.

"I haven't had a chance to tell you how much you helped me, Steve," Colonel Primrose said. "—Did you know it was Ridley?"

Steve shook his head with a grin. "I just didn't like his face. I didn't even know what was up, but I saw you move, and I figured you might need a little help."

"He'd have drunk it himself if you hadn't got him," Colonel Primrose said. He looked around. Lisa and Mrs. Ridley were coming down the dock, Lisa in blue jeans and a white shirt open at the throat. He turned back to Steve.

"You're actually going to let Miss Cecily out of your sight? I wouldn't."

Cecily looked up at Steve.

"The Lone Ranger returns to the wilderness," she laughed.

"Just till the end of summer," Steve grinned. "A job's a job. And it won't be wilderness . . . now."

His hands tightened on her shoulders under the stiff oilskin coat.

"You'll come to Cinnabar, soon?"

"The day the dudes leave the Park," he said. He lifted her lightly down into the waiting boat and jumped in beside her.

The elegant little craft shot out into the water. Mrs. Ridley and Bill were in front, going for the ride, to return that night; Lisa going to Cinnabar with Cecily and her grandmother, and Monty, who'd wangled a trip as far as the boundary to make the annual swan count. The swan, I suspected, was in the end seat beside him at the moment—converted from an ugly duckling in a twinkling of the eye. We watched the boat skim across the water, throwing up a barrage of silver spray. Bill's remark the night before came back to me.

"Gee, it's swell Monty's going back East to college this fall. He'll see Lisa every weekend. He's nuts about her. He said it didn't make any difference to him if she did have a lot of money."

"That's big of him," I said.

Bill ignored that. "I think a guy's a sap to think a girl like Cecily'd want to marry a dope like George and walk out so he could, don't you?"

Colonel Primrose and I watched the boat until it was a tiny dot disappearing into the hazy distance, into the dun-colored rim of mountains beyond. Beyond that was Thorofare. In an hour they'd meet Joe and the cook and the pack train at the Cabin Creek cabin, and spend the night again under the snowshoe cabin in the wilderness . . . but the tiny clearing in the pine woods wouldn't be lonely that night.

"Well, that's that," I said.

Colonel Primrose smiled.

"I suppose it is," he said. "The Winstons have pulled out too. Nice people."

We started back up to the hotel. "By the way," I said, "I've never understood why none of them showed, when George was shot."

"I didn't either, at first," he answered. "The fact is, Mrs. Ridley made them promise not to come out no matter what seemed to happen. Dick did come out, he says—saw all of us and went back. They were pretty scared. Thought Mrs. Ridley had done it."

"And how was it done, really?" I asked. "And how did you know?"

He shook his head. "It's not a pretty story, my dear. I pieced most of it together, and Ridley's ego was enough to make him glad to correct me at points. He came out here to kill George, of course, if it turned out to be necessary. George had phoned him from Cinnabar. He was doing so well with Cecily that he planned to stay out all summer, and he wanted Ridley to do some business for him. Ridley had no intention, at any time, of letting George marry. Of course the idea of George passing up a good deal of money by not having children wasn't like George. And Ridley had brought Lisa up under his heel so that when she was twenty-one all he'd have to do was collect, what with her and her mother. He enjoyed working on them, of course, even apart from the money, being a polite sadist.

"So, he carried those pills about for George. Then things moved so fast here, and worked out so well, that he decided to let Mrs. Ridley take the rap. Your being put in next to them made it a natural."

I shook my head ruefully. "I think I'll give up eavesdropping," I said. "It isn't ladylike."

He chuckled. "It's very useful. It saved Mrs. Ridley's life. It also confused me for a while."

I looked at him.

"—Until I thought of the obvious point. If you could hear him, he could hear you and know you could hear him . . . and I thought, when you told me about it, that it was a little odd he'd start making speeches to his wife. It was the plainest kind of a build-up, when you got to thinking about it. He obviously wasn't concerned with George's happiness . . . and the doubtful advantage of being connected with Chapman—George being the kind of fellow he was—just as obviously didn't outweigh having several millions turned loose in his family.

"Well, George hot-footed it to Ridley the night Mrs. Chapman invited him to join her at the Lodge. Ridley went back to his room with him and took his gun. He'd overheard Mrs. Chapman fixing the night watchman not to be around, and took advantage of it. He went along with George, out the end door, and shot him. He dropped his wife's clip there—she'd left the hotel in such a frenzy she didn't know she hadn't got it on. He heard Anders coming along, ducked behind the first trailer, and saw Mrs. Ridley come out. The ironic thing is that she didn't see him. She thought it was the Chapman crowd, until he gave himself away."

We'd got back up to the hotel. I stopped to speak to a woman and Colonel Primrose went on into the lounge. Just then I saw Pearl and Sergeant Phineas T. Buck coming along from a stroll in the woods, and I heard her say—apropos of what I wouldn't know—"You were just wonderful, Mr. Buck. I mean it, honestly."

I hurried on inside. Colonel Primrose was waiting for me at the end of the lounge, lighting a cigar. I sat down beside him, and I said, "You're just wonderful, Colonel Primrose. I mean it, honestly."

His cigar stopped dead half-way to his mouth. He looked at me in blank amazement.

"I've just decided to adopt Pearl's tactics," I said. "I'm going to be a lady hereafter, if it kills me."

He looked relieved, and finished lighting his cigar.

"Oddly enough, that's what sold Buck down the river," he said dryly. "I don't want you to take this as any kind of a reflection on you, but he's told me a dozen times she's a lady. Well, I suspect she is, drunk or sober."

I nodded complete agreement. "And how did you find out all the things you told Mrs. Chapman, that day in her room?"

He chuckled.

"There's a well-known outdoor sport in Yellowstone, my dear, called rotten-logging. They called it spooning in my day, and necking in yours. I don't know what it is in Bill's. One of the chamber maids and your admirer the bellboy saw Anders take the car and pick up Mrs. Chapman. They heard the shot, but she comes from Chicago and he was on duty at the elevator, and they were sitting in the manager's car. So they preferred to say nothing about it.—Actually, of course, we didn't have much evidence against Ridley, for the first murder. The thing that convinced me was when he lashed out at us as she was on the point of admitting she'd come out of the trailer. I needn't say I didn't realize you were as close to danger as you were—because I don't think Mr. Alexander Ridley would have hesitated to get rid of you if he'd had to. And oddly enough, I'm very fond of you."

Colonel Primrose smiled, and then, as he looked out the side window, his face clouded. I looked out too, and saw Pearl taking Sergeant Buck's picture.

That afternoon in Yellowstone will live long in my memory, for the reason that it accomplished, simply and unexpectedly and inexorably, the jettisoning of that lady known as Pearl. The particularly satisfactory thing about it was that nobody was responsible except Pearl herself. Not, of course, that Colonel Primrose and I hadn't done our best, but our best hadn't been good enough. We should have realized that in Nature's Wonderland nature should have been allowed to take her course . . . for that was precisely what happened.

It must have been about three o'clock when Pearl and the Sergeant set off, in the Sergeant's car, for a sight-seeing tour, and not long after that that Colonel Primrose suggested we might drive over and see Old Faithful operate, which I hadn't done. We set out in Mrs. Chapman's big car, along the Lake, stopping to look at the Grand Tetons rising up in white-peaked majesty beyond the southern rim of the lake, making a tour of the hot spots (just geysers) at West Thumb, and proceeding along the gorgeous drive across the Continental Divide. It was at the tiny twin lakes on the Divide, with their thick mantle of yellow water lilies, that we came to what in

Yellowstone is known as a bear jam. A sleek black mother bear with two enchanting cubs was entertaining a dozen cars. Half a dozen tourists were out tossing them bits of food—in spite of all warnings and regulations—and taking snapshots to show their friends at home.

The car just ahead of us was Sergeant Buck's. Pearl spotted us and came back smiling. Sergeant Buck followed, rock-ribbed and stony. A car drew up behind us and a girl got out. As she passed, Pearl said, "Just look at those finger nails. Personally, I don't think any real lady makes her nails that terrible red, do you, Colonel Primrose?"

Then she looked at me. "Oh, I beg your pardon, Mrs. Latham. I didn't notice yours."

"Oh, don't mind me," I said. Her own neatly cared-for nails on the side of the car were the palest pink. Only a woman's eye could spot the little line of dark red polish that she hadn't been able to get off.

"It's just that personally I don't think men like it," she said, Sergeant Buck looking at her with open admiration.

Then she turned to the performing animals. "I'm going to take a picture of that sweet little bear." She skipped away in her pink slacks, very lightly, really—for one of her size.

Sergeant Buck cleared his iron throat.

"I just wanted to say, sir," he said, out of the corner of his mouth, "—if you was thinking of getting married, sir, I was thinking of doing likewise."

Colonel Primrose, I must say, took it like an officer and a gentleman. The shock of it, if it was a shock at this point, was quite imperceptible.

"That's fine, Buck," he said, and held out his hand.

Sergeant Buck spat on a lily pad in the Great Divide, and reached out his tremendous fist.

"She's a lady, sir," he said simply. He looked at me, his eyes congealing. I avoided his glance, the implication being only too obvious, and looked around at Pearl.

Her back was to us, and she was bending over her camera, levelled low down at one of the cubs, seated on his haunches like an over-size teddy bear, his paws bent forward, posing like the professional he was rapidly becoming. It was too bad that just at that moment his mother, her forefeet on the window of a car behind Pearl, should have glanced around. Pearl's rear elevation, bent over, was not unrotund, and certainly not transparent—and the mother bear, confronted with a large pink mass between her and her child, which is what *all* the books about Yellowstone say must not happen, turned rapidly, and made one lunge at Pearl, and one slash.

Her claws raked in, a little, and Pearl, not hurt really but scared out of her wits, made a violent terrified lurch forward, and spun around, and said, very feelingly . . .

But a lady couldn't repeat—having never before heard —the things Pearl called that bear.

Sergeant Buck, half way across the Great Divide to her rescue, stopped as if a thunderbolt had struck him square between the eyes. He stood there for a moment, a granite avalanche miraculously stopped motionless and rooted. Then he turned his head and spat, on the road this time. He came back to the car, leaving Pearl, yammering like a fish-wife, surrounded by frightened tourists. The mother bear and her cubs were streaking across the Divide at full speed ahead, making for the deep timber.

Sergeant Buck's lantern-jawed dead pan was a grim relic of the last ice age. He looked at the Colonel silently for an instant. He cleared his throat.

"I . . . expect I was a damn fool, sir," he said, out of the corner of his mouth.

"Well," Colonel Primrose said, tentatively but politely.

Sergeant Buck cleared his throat again. For the moment he looked like an unhappy fossilized mountain sheep.

"Irregardless of what you was planning, sir," he said, "I'm done with women, personally."